The Singing Sack

28 song-stories from around the world

Compiled by Helen East
at the National Folktale Centre

Illustrated by Mary Currie

A & C Black · London

Contents

First published 1989 by A & C Black (Publishers) Ltd
35 Bedford Row, London WC1R 4JH
Reprinted 1991, 1992
Compilation © 1989 Helen East
Illustrations © 1989 Mary Currie

ISBN 0 7136 3115 5

Music set by Linda Lancaster
Printed in Great Britain by Hollen Street Press Ltd,
Slough, Berkshire

A CIP catalogue record for this book is available from the British Library.

Introduction

I hope that you will enjoy these song-stories and learn to sing and tell them.

A story which contains a song lingers in the memory and pleases the ear in a different way from pure narrative; the song adds a special element and gives a particular atmosphere to the story. Often it is repeated or has a simple chorus which gives an opportunity for everyone to participate, making the storytelling into a properly communal and lively event.

Most of the song-stories have been transcribed from live storytellings. They were gathered together at the National Folktale Centre, a charity which both collects folktales and encourages their continuance in the oral tradition.

A few of the stories are my own retellings of tales, heard in childhood, or rediscovered in old editions of stories. Some had lost their original melodies and as far as possible I have traced the original tunes. But in a few cases I have found substitutes from the appropriate tradition.

Most of the songs are given in their original language which fits the rhythm of the melody in a way which English often cannot; in many places it also provides alliteration and onomatopoeia. It helps children to tune their ears to different languages, if they learn to sing them. They

very soon pick up the sounds aided by the rhythm of the song. Occasionally a singable English version is included, when this has been given by the storyteller.

The cassette which accompanies the book has been recorded with repeats to match those in the story. It can be played during the telling of a story. But it will also help you to sing the songs yourselves, so dispense with the cassette as soon as you feel confident enough.

The stories come from the mouths of storytellers – they are meant to be told live, not left on the page. Put the book down sometimes and try it for yourself. Retell the tales in your own words, dramatise them, stop and ask the children what happens next, let *them* find a solution to the dilemma in which *The Blind Beggar* finds himself, or try to collect the water while *Spider the Drummer* is playing his entrancing music. Make them your own, as generations of storytellers have done before you.

My special thanks go to Ian Rankin for all the transcribing, typing, tea-making and advice; to Sheena Roberts for singing, researching, editing and arranging; to Rick Wilson for technical and moral support, and to all the many people who helped put this book together.

Helen East
Director of the National Folktale Centre

Gluskabi and the Wind Eagle

Long ago, Gluskabi lived with his grandmother, Woodchuck, in a small lodge beside the big water. One day Gluskabi was walking around when he looked out and saw some ducks in the bay.

'I think it is time to go hunt some ducks,' he said. So he took his bow and arrows and got into his canoe. He began to paddle out into the bay and as he paddled he sang:

> **Ki yo wah ji neh**
> **Yo ho hui ho,**
> **Ki yo wah ji neh**
> **Ki yo wah ji neh.**
> **Ki yo wah ji neh**
> **Yo ho hui,**
> **Ki yo wah ji neh**
> **Ki yo wah ji neh.** (*Sing three times*)

But a wind came up and it turned his canoe and blew him back to shore. Once again Gluskabi began to paddle out and this time he sang his song a little harder:

KI YO WAH JI NEH . . .

But again the wind came and blew him back to shore. Four times he tried to paddle out into the bay and four times he failed.

He was not happy.

He went back to the lodge of his grandmother and walked right in, even though there was a stick leaned across the door, which meant that the person inside was doing some work and did not want to be disturbed.

'Grandmother,' Gluskabi said, 'what makes the wind blow?'

Grandmother Woodchuck looked up from her work. 'Gluskabi,' she said, 'why do you want to know?'

Then Gluskabi answered her just as every child in the world does when they are asked such a question.

'Because,' he said.

Grandmother Woodchuck looked at him. 'Ah, Gluskabi,' she said, 'whenever you ask

such questions I feel there is going to be trouble. And perhaps I should not tell you. But I know that you are so stubborn you will never stop asking until I answer you. So, I shall tell you. Far from here, on top of the tallest mountain, a great bird stands. This bird is named Wuchowsen and when he flaps his wings, he makes the wind blow.'

'Eh-hey, Grandmother,' said Gluskabi. 'I see. Now how would one find that place where the Wind Eagle stands?'

Again Grandmother Woodchuck looked at Gluskabi. 'Ah, Gluskabi,' she said, 'once again I feel that perhaps I should not tell you. But I know that you are very stubborn and would never stop asking. So, I shall tell you. If you walk always facing the wind you will come to the place where Wuchowsen stands.'

'Thank you, Grandmother,' said Gluskabi. He stepped out of the lodge and faced into the wind and began to walk.

He walked across the fields and through the woods and the wind blew hard. He walked through the valleys and into the hills and the wind blew harder still. He came to the foothills and began to climb and the wind still blew harder. Now the foothills were becoming mountains and the wind was very strong. Soon there were no longer any trees and the wind was very, very strong. The wind was so strong that it blew off Gluskabi's mokasins. But he was very stubborn and he kept on walking, leaning into the wind. Now the wind was so strong that it blew off his shirt, but he kept on walking. Now the wind was so strong that it blew off all his clothes and he was naked, but he still kept walking. Now the wind was so strong that it blew off his hair, but Gluskabi still kept walking, facing into the wind. The wind was so strong that it blew off his eyebrows, but still he continued to walk. Now the wind was so strong that he could hardly stand. He had to pull himself along by grabbing hold of the boulders. But there, on the peak ahead of him, he could see a great bird slowly flapping its wings. It was Wuchowsen, the Wind Eagle.

Gluskabi took a deep breath. 'GRANDFATHER!' he shouted.

The Wind Eagle stopped flapping his wings and looked around. 'Who calls me Grandfather?' he said.

Gluskabi stood up. 'It's me, Grandfather. I just came up here to tell you that you do a very good job making the wind blow.'

The Wind Eagle puffed out his chest with pride. 'You mean like this?' he said and he flapped his wings even harder. The wind which he made was so strong that it lifted Gluskabi right off his feet and he would have been blown right off the mountain had he not reached out and grabbed a boulder again.

'GRANDFATHER!!!' Gluskabi shouted again.

The Wind Eagle stopped flapping his wings. 'Yesss?' he said.

Gluskabi stood up and came closer to Wuchowsen. 'You do a very good job of making the wind blow, Grandfather. This is so. But it seems to me that you could do an even better job if you were on that other peak over there.'

The Wind Eagle looked towards the other peak. 'That may be so,' he said, 'but how would I get from here to there?'

Gluskabi smiled. 'Grandfather,' he said. 'I will carry you. Wait here.'

Then Gluskabi ran back down the mountain until he came to a big basswood

tree. He stripped off the outer bark and from the inner bark he braided a strong carrying strap which he took back up the mountain to the Wind Eagle. 'Here, Grandfather,' he said, 'let me wrap this around you so I can lift you more easily.'

Then he wrapped the carrying strap so tightly around Wuchowsen that his wings were pulled in to his sides and he could hardly breathe.

'Now, Grandfather,' Gluskabi said, picking the Wind Eagle up, 'I will take you to a better place.'

He began to walk towards the other peak, but as he walked he came to a place where there was a large crevice and as he stepped over it he let go of the carrying strap and the Wind Eagle slid down into the crevice, upside-down, and was stuck.

'Now,' Gluskabi said, 'it is time to hunt some ducks.'

He walked back down the mountain and there was no wind at all. He walked till he came to the treeline and still no wind blew. He walked down to the foothills and down to the hills and the valleys and still there was no wind. He walked through the forests and through the fields and the wind did not blow at all. He walked and walked until he came back to the lodge by the water and by now all his hair had grown back. He put on some fine new clothing and a new pair of mokasins and took his bow and arrows and went down to the bay and climbed into his boat to hunt ducks. He paddled out into the water and sang another canoeing song:

Ya nay ho
Gai yo ha nay ho,
Hey yoo
Gai yo wa nay ho,
Hey ya gai yo wah ney ho
Hey ya gai yo wah ney ho.
(*Sing three times*)

But the air was very hot and still, and he began to sweat. The air was so still and hot that it was hard to breathe. Soon the water began to grow dirty and smell bad, and there was so much foam on the water he could hardly paddle. He was not pleased at all and he returned to shore and went straight to his Grandmother's lodge and walked in.

'Grandmother,' he said, 'what is wrong? The air is hot and still and it is making me sweat and it is hard to breathe. The water is dirty and covered with foam. I cannot hunt ducks at all like this.'

Grandmother Woodchuck looked up at Gluskabi. 'Gluskabi,' she said, 'what have you done now?'

And Gluskabi answered just as every child in the world answers when asked that question.

'Oh, nothing,' he said.

'*Gluskabi*,' said Grandmother Woodchuck again, 'tell me what you have done.'

Then Gluskabi told her about going to visit the Wind Eagle and what he had done to stop the wind.

'Oh, Gluskabi,' said Grandmother Woodchuck, 'will you never learn?

Tabaldak, the Owner, set the Wind Eagle on that mountain to make the wind because we need the wind. The wind keeps the air cool and clean. The wind brings the clouds which give us rain to wash the earth. The wind moves the waters and keeps them fresh and sweet. Without the wind, life will not be good for us or for our children or our children's children.'

Gluskabi nodded his head. 'Kaamoji, Grandmother,' he said. 'I understand.'

Then he went outside. He faced in the direction from which the wind had once come and began to walk. He walked through the fields and through the forests and the wind did not blow and he felt very hot. He walked through the valleys and up the hills and there was no wind and it was hard for him to breathe. He came to the foothills and began to climb and he was very hot and sweaty indeed. At last he came to the mountain where the Wind Eagle once stood and he went and looked down into the crevice. There Wuchowsen the Wind Eagle was, wedged upside down.

'Uncle?' Gluskabi called.

The Wind Eagle looked up as best he could. 'Who calls me Uncle?' he said.

'It is Gluskabi, Uncle. I'm up here. But what are you doing down there?'

'Oh, Gluskabi,' said the Wind Eagle, 'a very ugly, naked man with no hair told me that he would take me to the other peak so that I could do a better job of making the wind blow. He tied my wings and picked me up, but as he stepped over this crevice he dropped me in and I am stuck. And I am not comfortable here at all.'

'Ah, Grandfath . . . er, Uncle, I will get you out.'

Then Gluskabi climbed down into the crevice. He pulled the Wind Eagle free and placed him back on his mountain and untied his wings.

'Uncle,' Gluskabi said, 'it is good that the wind should blow sometimes and other times it is good that it should be still.'

The Wind Eagle looked at Gluskabi and then nodded his head. 'Grandson,' he said, 'I hear what you say.'

So it is that sometimes there is wind and sometimes it is still to this very day. And so the story goes.

The Finger Lock

There were three brothers, the MacCrimmons, and they lived in a cottage away on a hill. The two elder brothers were very good pipers, but the youngest, wee Johnnie, couldn't play at all. They didn't give him a chance; they kept him too busy slaving away for them. He had to do all the work: tending the fire, cooking the food, washing the dishes and everything.

Now it happened one year, the elder brothers were getting ready to go to the Games, where there was a big piping competition. Poor Johnnie, he had to run round shining up their belts and buckles and medals, so they'd look fine and smart. And *he* wanted to go to the games too, to hear his brothers and all the other great pipers play. He begged and he pleaded.

'I've never been,' he said, 'never in my life. Please let me come with you tomorrow.'

But his brothers just gave him a slap. 'Be quiet,' they said, 'and get on with your work. You've got to take the cows down to the water, and clean out the byre. You don't have time to come, and anyway, you look such a mess, we don't want you with us.'

So the next day his brothers gave Johnnie a long list of work to do, and they locked him out of the house too, so he couldn't go and help himself to food or anything. And then off they went in the pony and trap with their pipes.

Johnnie was broken-hearted. He took the cows down to the water, and he sat and watched over them, as miserable as anything. And then, suddenly, he heard a little voice saying, 'Johnnie. What's wrong? You look awful down-hearted.'

Johnnie looked down, and he saw a fairy, a wee green man, sitting there cross-legged looking at him.

'Well,' said Johnnie, 'it's my brothers. They won't let me go to the Games and hear the pipers. And they hit me, too.'

'Never mind,' said the fairy, 'I'll play you a tune or two.'

'But you don't have any pipes,' said Johnnie.

'Never mind that either,' said the fairy. 'Just find me a straw, and that will do for me.'

So Johnnie found him a straw, and the little man put it in his mouth, and played it like the pipes. And he played the loveliest reels and tunes you ever heard in your life:

The Fairy Dance

After a while the fairy stopped and said, 'Now it's your turn. Go and get dressed and then off you go and play the pipes at the Games.'

'But I can't play a note,' said Johnnie. 'Not even on the chanter. And I'm locked out of the house too.'

'Never mind that,' said the fairy. 'Just

The Fairy Dance (A drone)

End

blow on the lock, then put your little finger into it and turn it like a key.'

Johnnie did what he was told, and sure enough the door opened.

'Now,' said the fairy, 'get the old chest from under your bed.'

'What old chest?' asked Johnnie.

'Just go and see,' said the fairy.

Sure enough again, when Johnnie went to look, there was an old chest. And inside, it was full to the brim with kilts, and buckles, and all he needed to wear, and right in the middle was a set of pipes. And these pipes were mounted in solid gold.

'But,' said Johnnie, 'I told you. I can't play. Not at all.'

'Just blow and try,' said the fairy.

So Johnnie put the pipes to his shoulder and tuned up. Then he began to play. And you never heard a piper play so well – to this day there has never been a piper to match Johnnie. Strathspeys, reels, pibroch, he played them all.

'Now,' said the fairy, 'you're ready. But when you get to the Games and you get on the stage, you must play a new tune. No one's ever heard it before. Just move your fingers and you'll play it, and you must call

the tune *The Finger Lock* to remind you of the way you unlocked your own door. And now here's your horse and trap, so off you go!'

So Johnnie did go to the Games after all, and he was just in time for the piping competition. He was the last piper to play. He got on the stage and he started to play, and everyone just stared and listened as if they were dreaming. And when he started to play *The Finger Lock*, the judges came crowding round; they'd never heard the like of it.

The Finger Lock

Of course he won all the prizes, but he didn't stay late. He hurried off home when no one was looking and hid the pipes and his clothes in the old chest. Then he put on his old rags and got on with his work. By and by his brothers came back, looking very tired and very bad-tempered.

'How did you get on today, brothers?' asked Johnnie, smiling to himself. 'Did you win any prizes?'

'Not a thing,' said his brothers. 'And we

The Finger Lock (A drone)

Spider the Drummer

won't go again! There was a lad there – you never heard anyone play like him. He took all the prizes. Not a piper in the world could beat that man. And he played a new tune – *The Finger Lock* – it was out of this world, that tune.'

'*The Finger Lock?*' said Johnnie. 'Is that all? I could play that tune myself. Give me your pipes and I'll play it to you.'

'Oh get out!' cried his brothers. 'You're daft! And leave our pipes alone!'

'All right,' said Johnnie, 'I'll get my own pipes.'

And he went and got the golden ones out of the chest, and tuned them up, and walked into the room playing. And his two brothers just sat there with their mouths open, watching him play.

From that day on, the two elder MacCrimmon brothers never went to any more pipe playing contests. But wee Johnnie did, he went to them all, and he was always the best, wherever he went. And his tune, *The Finger Lock* is still played to this day. And that's the truth.

Once upon a time, when spiders and animals could talk, they used to live all together with people. In this one village there was to be a wedding party. Before the wedding started, they had to invite the guests and the musicians. Of course, Spider was the best musician, because he had eight legs and he used all of them to play instruments all at the same time.

But there were doubts about inviting Spider. For one thing, if Spider went to a party, his wife and all his children went too, and they would sit down and eat up everything, regardless of what the other guests thought of them: they ate *everything* in sight! This had been going on for years and years, and people were getting really fed up of Spider eating everything, so this time they decided not to invite him, and not even to tell him about the party.

So the news went around that there was to be a party, but that nobody was to tell Spider about it. However, Spider being a man of the town, someone somewhere told him about the party, and he was really furious because he was the best musician and he was everybody's friend – so why had no one invited him? He decided that he

would have his revenge – but how? He had to work out the answer to that, and, cunning as he was, he found a very crafty way of doing it.

Shall I tell you about the village? In this village, they didn't have water-taps like we do in modern times. Instead, they had a stream where everyone went to fetch water. All around this stream were tall trees and thick, thick grasses, so very little sunlight got through there. Well, in the night, when everyone was asleep, Spider called to his children and his wife and he said, 'You see what they've done? They haven't invited us to the wedding party. Well, we're going to teach them all a lesson.'

He called all his children, and they took the best of his drums and musical instruments and went down to the stream and hid them behind a bush. Then Spider, his wife and his children waited there all night hidden in the long grass.

Next morning, the party started. Everyone went to the village quietly, not passing in front of Spider's house so that they wouldn't wake him up. They arrived at the place where the party was to be held and started to get things ready. Before the cooking could start, however, they needed water, and the youngest girl was told to fetch some. So the girl took a calabash, which is a sort of pail, and went down to the stream.

Well, as soon as she dipped the calabash into the water, strange music began to play. It seemed to come from everywhere, from all directions at once, wild drumming and singing, echoing through the forest:

Pijin do me so congo a yehreh,
   a yehreh congo,
Pijin do me so congo a yehreh,
   a yehreh congo,
Pijin do me so congo a yehreh,
   a yehreh congo . . .
(Repeat ad lib)

It was so beautiful, she felt happy and started to dance, but once she had started to dance she found she couldn't stop. She danced and danced and danced until she fell to the ground exhausted.

Everybody was waiting back at the party, and eventually the hostess said, 'Send someone else to fetch that girl, and bring some water back with them.'

So somebody, a boy this time, went to find the girl. The music had stopped by the time he reached the stream, but the girl was still lying there dazed. The boy asked what had happened, and she said: 'Look, when I put my calabash in the water, this music started, I don't know from where, and I started to dance.'

Then the boy said, 'You must be lying. I can't hear any music, and I can't see anyone. Why are you lying? Give the calabash to me, let's get the water and go back to the party.'

So the boy tipped the calabash into the stream, and the music started again:

Pijin do me so congo a yehreh,
   a yehreh congo . . .
(Repeat ad lib)

Pi - jin do me so con - go a yeh - reh, a yeh - reh con - go.

SECOND VOICE

Pi - jin do me so con - go a yeh - reh, a yeh - reh con - go.

And the boy started dancing and dancing, and it went on for hours.

Meanwhile, the hostess was getting cross. 'What has happened?' she said. 'How can we cook when no one has come back with any water?'

So it was decided to send another person, and then another, and another, until *everyone* who'd been at the party was at the stream, dancing their heads off! So the hostess decided to go down to the stream herself, and she too started dancing and couldn't stop:

**Pijin do me so congo a yehreh,
    a yehreh congo . . .**
(*Repeat ad lib*)

Eventually, somebody got their breath and started using their brain.

'Who on earth could be playing such hypnotic music?' he asked.

'It must be Spider,' someone said. 'Where *is* Spider? Spider's not here! Did no one invite him?'

'No.'

'Oh gracious me, then that's the answer! If Spider wasn't invited, he'd definitely do something like this. I know him.'

So then everyone started to shout for Spider to come out, and Spider appeared from some bushes and said, 'Yes, it's me.'

'Why are you doing this to us?' everyone asked.

'Don't you know that you didn't invite me to your party?' said Spider. 'Ah yes, you forgot. So I decided to catch you all here, hypnotised by my music, and bring the party to a standstill. And I'll start playing again!'

'No,' they begged, 'please don't start the music again. What do you want from us?'

'You know what I want,' said Spider. 'Take me back to the party and let me eat all I can, feed my eight legs and my children and my wife.'

And they said, 'Spider, look, we can't invite you if you are going to eat everything, so if we *do* invite you, will you promise to eat only some and leave some for the rest of us?'

But Spider wouldn't agree, and soon they had to give in, or they would be stuck fast by the riverside. And so Spider was invited to the party after all, and everyone had a good time. You know, Spider will never change his ways, and that's the end of my story!

Quilla Bung

One day, a man and his wife had nothing to eat for dinner. So the man went out with his gun to see if he could shoot something. As he was going along he heard a song:

Laleelu come quilla, come quilla,
Bung, bung, bung quilla bung.

He looked up, and what did he see? A whole flock of geese flying overhead, and they were all singing. The man licked his lips, lifted his gun, aimed, fired, and BANG! he shot one. But as it fell down from the sky, it sang:

Laleelu come quilla, come quilla,
Bung, bung, bung quilla bung.

He took it home and gave it to his wife to cook. She laid it down, and began to pluck it. But every feather she plucked flew out of her hand and floated out the window. And all the while, the goose kept singing:

Laleelu come quilla, come quilla,
Bung, bung, bung quilla bung.

Well, she finished at last, and she put the goose in the stove to cook it. But all the time it was cooking, she could hear in muffled tones from inside the stove:

Laleelu come quilla, come quilla,
Bung, bung, bung quilla bung.

Anyway, they sat down to dinner, the husband and wife, and she put the goose on the table between them. And the man picked up the carving knife to carve it, but all the while it sang:

Laleelu come quilla, come quilla,
Bung, bung, bung quilla bung.

And as he held up the carving fork ready to stick into the goose, there came a tremendous noise. In through the window flew the whole flock of geese, and they were all singing as loud as could be:

Laleelu come quilla, come quilla,
Bung, bung, bung quilla bung.

Then each one took out a feather, and stuck it into the goose, and then all together they lifted that goose right out of the dish. And up it flew and followed them, and round they went and out the window.

And the man and his wife sat there with empty plates and open mouths, and stared. But all they got for dinner that night was a song!

Laleelu come quilla, come quilla,
Bung, bung, bung quilla bung.
Laleelu come quilla, come quilla,
Bung, bung, bung quilla bung.
Laleelu come quilla, come quilla,
Bung, bung, bung quilla bung.
Laleelu come quilla . . .
(*Repeat, gradually fading.*)

Nyangara the Python

Once upon a time there was a Chief who had, as his medical advisor, a python, whose name was Nyangara.

Now one day this Chief fell very sick indeed, so he called the men of his village together and he said, 'My men, I am very sick ... and I fear ... I may die ... if I do not see ... my doctor. Go up ... all of you ... to the cave ... on the top of the hill ... where my python lives ... my doctor ... Nyangara. And sing him ... the magic song ... which you know ... Then he will come ... out of his cave ... and you will bring him ... to me. When you go ... take a pot of beer ... as a present ... from me.'

So the men did as they were told. They climbed up to the top of the hill, stood outside the cave of Nyangara the Python, and sang him the magic song:

Nyangara, chena, Nyangara, chena,
Nyangara, chena, Nyangara, chena,
Nyangara, chena, Nyangara, chena,
Nyangara, chena. Nyangara, chena ...
(*Repeat ad lib*)

(Nyangara, come out. Nyangara, come out ...)

CHORUS

Nyan - ga - ra,   che - na,

Repeat ad lib

Nyan - ga - ra,   che - na.

But when Nyangara heard his song, and began to uncoil two, three, four coils, the men were so frightened that they dropped the pot of beer, and they ran away.

Then they went back to the Chief and said, 'We are very sorry, Chief, but you will have to die without your doctor, as we are too frightened to bring him to you.'

Now the Chief was very sad indeed that no one was brave enough to bring him his python.

But the little children of the village heard what the men had done, and they said to each other, 'Let us go up the hill to fetch Nyangara the Python, the Chief's doctor.'

So they went to the Chief and they said, 'Father, let us go up the hill to fetch your doctor.'

And the Chief said, 'Thank you ... my children. I will teach you ... the magic song ... which you must sing ... outside the cave ... of Nyangara.'

So he taught them the song, and he said, 'Now ... my children ... you must take ... another pot of beer ... to my doctor ... as a present ... from me.'

So, twenty little children took the pot of beer and set off. Up, up, up they climbed, right up to the top of the hill and they stood in a row outside the cave of the python and began to sing:

Nai-we Nyangara-we,
Ta zo ku wona, Nyangara.

Nai-we Nyangara-we,
Mambo wedu wofa, Nyangara.

(*Chorus sung throughout*):
Nyangara, chena. Nyangara, chena ...

(Please, please, Nyangara-we,
We want to see you, Nyangara.

Please, please, Nyangara-we,
Our chief is dying, Nyangara.

Chorus
Nyangara, come out. Nyangara, come out ...)

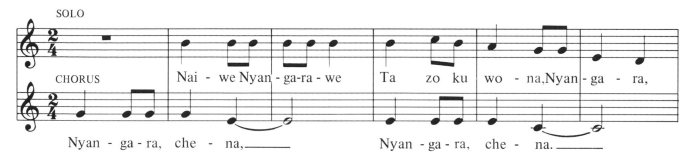

SOLO

CHORUS

Nai - we Nyan - ga-ra-we Ta zo ku wo -na, Nyan - ga - ra,

Nyan - ga - ra, che - na, _____ Nyan - ga - ra, che - na. _____

Repeat ad lib

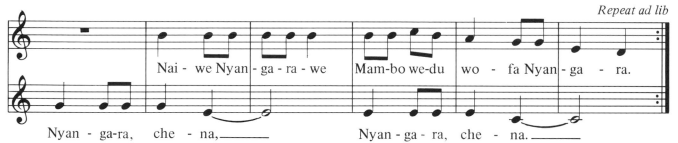

Nai - we Nyan - ga - ra - we Mam-bo we-du wo - fa Nyan - ga - ra.

Nyan - ga - ra, che - na, _____ Nyan - ga - ra, che - na. _____

And the python answered them from within, saying: 'Yes, yes, children of the Chief. Climb up here. Others came here only yesterday. Ha-a-ia, climb up here. They broke the pot of beer and ran away. Are you going to run away?'

But the children stood stock still and went on singing:

Nai-we Nyangara-we,
Ta zo ku wona, Nyangara . . .

Nyangara, chena . . .

And then the python began to uncoil himself and come out of the cave. He uncoiled three . . . four . . . six . . . seven . . . nine, all ten coils, and came right out of his cave. Then he curled himself up onto the shoulders of nineteen little children, and the twentieth walked in front with the pot of beer on his head, out of which the python drank as they went along. So they brought him down, down the hill to the Chief's hut. And they put him down outside the door. They opened the door and

looked inside, and there was the Chief, lying on his mat, and he was very sick indeed. Then the python went inside the hut and they shut the door after him. So Nyangara the Python set about the Chief at once. He licked him all over his back, down his legs, up his front, and all over his face; and when he had finished licking his face, the Chief woke up, quite well again, and he said, 'Thank you, my python, for coming to see me. Now I'll send you back to your home in the cave.'

So he called the little children and said, 'Take my python, my Nyangara, back to his cave on top of the hill, and when you go, take him an ox as a present from me.'

So the little children took Nyangara back to his cave. And when they came back, the Chief said, 'Now, my children, you can take another ox for yourselves, and have a feast of meat. But don't you let the grown-ups have any, for they would have let me die.'

And that was the end of that story.

The Lonely Mermaid

There was a fisherman one time, and he lived on one of the little islands off the coast of Scotland.

One day he was out with his nets and he caught something very heavy. And when he pulled it up, he saw that it was a mermaid. She was so lovely, as soon as he looked at her he fell in love with her. And although she begged and pleaded with him to let her go back to her home in the water, he wouldn't listen. He took off her 'slough' (her mermaid's tail) so she couldn't swim any more, and he brought her home to his island and made her his wife. As for the tail, he hid that away carefully at the back of an old barn, where he was sure she would never find it.

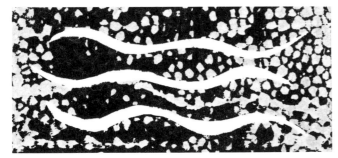

Time passed, and she had two children, both strong and bonny boys. But the mermaid still missed her old life. She sat for hours looking out to sea, and sang sad songs to herself as she worked. In those days on the island they didn't grow crops, so they didn't have any straw to use as bedding for the animals and themselves. So the women had to cut bracken to use instead, and that was hard and tiring work. And as she cut the bracken, the mermaid used to sing:

I'm so weary all alone,
Pulling bracken, pulling bracken,
I'm so weary all alone,
Pulling bracken early.
  Pulling bracken, pulling bracken,
  Pulling bracken early,
  Pulling bracken, pulling bracken,
  Pulling bracken early.

Tha mi sgìth, 's mi leam fhìn,
Buain na rainich, buain na rainich,
Tha mi sgìth, 's mi leam fhìn,
Buain na rainich m'ònar.
  Buain na rainich, buain na rainich,
  Buain na rainich m'ònar.
  Buain na rainich, buain na rainich,
  Buain na rainich m'ònar.

She was very unhappy and very lonely. But the children and her husband didn't pay any attention to her: they didn't understand, you see.

Then one day, when the husband was out fishing, one of the wee boys was playing in the barn and he found the 'slough' which the fisherman had hidden. He didn't know what it was, so he went running in to show it to his mammy. And the moment she saw it, she couldn't stop herself. She put it on and jumped into the sea.

When the fisherman came home and heard what had happened, he was heartbroken. He ran down to the waterside, calling and shouting and crying for her. Then at last he saw her, sitting on a rock right away out, and he heard her singing:

I'm so weary all alone . . .

Tha mi sgìth . . .

I'm so wea-ry all a-lone,
Tha mi sgìth,___ 's m leam fhìn,
Ha mee skee,___ smee lam heen,

Pull-ing bra-cken, pull-ing bra-cken,
Buain na rain-ich, buain na rain-ich,
Boo-ine na ran-ich, boo-ine na ran-ich,

I'm so wea-ry all a-lone,
Tha mi sgìth___ 's m leam fhìn,
Ha mee skee___ smee lam heen,

Pull-ing bra-cken ear-ly.
Buain na rain-ich m'òn-ar.
Boo-ine na ran-ich mo-nar.

Pull-ing bra-cken, pull-ing bra-cken,
Buain na rain-ich, buain na rain-ich,
Boo-ine na ran-ich, boo-ine na ran-ich,

Pull-ing bra-cken ear-ly,
Buain na rain-ich m'òn-ar,
Boo-ine na ran-ich mo-nar,

Pull-ing bra-cken, pull-ing bra-cken,
Buain na rain-ich, buain na rain-ich,
Boo-ine na ran-ich, boo-ine na ran-ich,

Pull-ing bra-cken ear-ly.
Buain na rain-ich m'òn-ar.
Boo-ine na ran-ich mo-nar.

ch as in Bach   ea in leam sounds between a and u

As she sang, the mermaid swam closer to him and beckoned. It was more than he could bear, and suddenly he jumped into the water and swam out to join her.

The children were left behind, but their granny lived nearby, so they were all right. They grew up and got married and had children themselves. And they say that these children, and their children too, walked like a mermaid would have done on land, or maybe like a seal would, flapping along. Right up to this day, there are supposed to be people on that island who walk like that.

Momo-taro-san

Have you ever heard a story about a baby boy found in the middle of a giant peach? Well, they have a tale like this in Japan, and they call the boy Momo-taro-san. He had lots of adventures, but the one I'm going to tell you about happened when he was about thirteen or fourteen years old.

At this time, Japan was having terrible problems. There were some horrible, monstrous demons living in a place called Demon Island, off the coast of Japan, and do you know the kind of things they did? If a boat came near their island, they would snatch it out of the sea and crush it, killing everyone on board, just for fun.

Well, Momo-taro-san decided that he was going to go and put a stop to these demons, but when he told his parents they were very worried, as you can imagine, because they knew it would be dangerous. They tried to persuade him to stay but he was determined to go.

The day came when he was to leave, and his parents cooked him some very special food for the journey. This food is called kibidango, and it's a sticky rice ball, very sweet and delicious. So he tied the kibidango on to his belt and set off down

the road, and his parents waved until they couldn't see him any more.

Now Momo-taro-san hadn't gone down the road very far when a pheasant came running out across his path. And this pheasant got half-way and then stopped, sniffed the air and said, 'Ooh, I can smell kibidango. It's my favourite food in the whole world.' And she sang this song:

Momo-taro-san, Momo-taro-san,
Okoshi ni tsuketa kibidango,
Hitotsu watashi ni kudasai na!

Now the words of this song mean, 'Momo-taro-san, please give me one of the kibidango on your waist.'

'Well!' said Momo-taro-san, 'I *will* give you one if you will help me fight the demons on Demon Island.'

'Oh yes, that's alright,' she said, 'I'll do anything for kibidango.'

And she followed him down the road.

They got a bit further when a dog came out from a ditch. He got half-way across the road, stopped, and began to whine and yelp. And what do you think he smelled?

That's right, the kibidango, and so he sang the song too:

Momo-taro-san, Momo-taro-san . . .

And Momo-taro-san said, 'You can have some kibidango if you come and help me fight the demons on Demon Island.'

Now the dog wasn't so very brave, but he thought that maybe he could just fight the small demons and leave the big ones for someone else. So he followed the pheasant, who followed Momo-taro-san, and they went on down the road.

And further along, there was a monkey in a tree, and he swung across the road to another branch, then suddenly raced down the trunk and came up to Momo-taro-san.

'I can smell Kibidango and it makes me so hungry!' he said.

And the monkey also sang this song:

Momo-taro-san, Momo-taro-san . . .

And what do you think Momo-taro-san said? Yes, 'You can have some if you help me fight the demons on Demon Island.'

Well, the monkey wasn't at all brave, but he thought if the fighting got too tough, he could hide in a tree until it was all over. So the monkey followed the dog, who followed the pheasant, who followed Momo-taro-san, and they went on down the road. They walked and they walked and at last they came to the sea.

There they found a fisherman, sitting sadly by his boat.

'What's wrong? Can we help?' asked Momo-taro-san.

'Ah, I wish you could,' said the fisherman. 'It's the demons, you see. I daren't take my boat out anymore, so I can't catch any fish, and my wife and children are very hungry. The whole village is suffering because we all rely on fish to eat.'

'Well, we've come to get rid of the demons once and for all,' said Momo-taro-san.

And the fisherman was so happy to hear this that he lent them his boat, and they started to row out across the sea. Soon they could see the island in the distance. As they got nearer, they could see a huge wall rising up as high as the tallest building you've ever seen. They tied up the boat and started to walk around the island, but the wall went all the way round. There was only one way in, a huge gate, but it was guarded by two of the most frightening, enormous, fierce demons that you've ever imagined in your worst nightmares; and each of them had two horns on his forehead.

'What are we going to do now?' wailed the monkey. 'We can't get through that gate with those two demons there.'

And they all shrank back behind a tree so that they wouldn't be seen. All except the pheasant, who started picking up stones from the ground in her beak. The others wondered what she was doing. Then she flew to the top of this high wall, and after a minute she took one of the stones in her beak, and do you know what she did? She spat it at one of those demon guards. It hit him right on the forehead. He looked all around but couldn't see anybody except the other guard. He glared at him and said, 'Why are you throwing stones at me?'

'I'm not throwing stones – don't be

stupid,' said the other guard.

'Don't call *me* stupid,' said the first guard and he started muttering to himself.

A moment later, the pheasant took up another stone in her beak and spat it at the other guard.

'I didn't throw a stone at you,' he said, 'so why are you throwing one at me now?'

'I didn't!'

'You did!'

'I didn't – what's the matter with you?'

'There's nothing the matter with me!'

And the *second* guard started pacing the ground and muttering to himself.

Just then, the pheasant picked up two more stones in her beak and she spat one at each guard.

'You threw another stone at me!'

'No, you threw one at me!'

'You throw stones and don't know you're doing it. There's something wrong with you!'

And they started to fight each other. But they were both exactly the same size and strength, and so neither of them could win. They just carried on punching and kicking, and the ground shook with their fighting, until they had knocked each other out and

they both fell unconscious to the ground.

Then the pheasant flew down to the inside of the gate and turned the key in the lock with her beak. In walked Momo-taro-san, the dog and the monkey. Well, what do you think the demons inside the wall were doing? They were all watching to see what was going to happen, because they'd felt the ground shake, and heard all the noise.

Momo-taro-san strode forward and proclaimed, 'I and my army have come to defeat you.'

When the demons saw that the army consisted of a dog, a monkey, and a pheasant, they all began to laugh, but it wasn't a pleasant sort of laughter, not at all the kind you'd enjoy hearing. Then, as Momo-taro-san and the animals stood watching, all these hideous and frightening demons, with horns growing from their foreheads, stood up and began to walk towards them. They got nearer and nearer,

but suddenly stopped, because over Momo-taro-san's shoulder do you know what they saw? Yes, the bodies of the two guards lying on the ground, looking for all the world as if they were dead.

'This boy must have some sort of magic powers if he can kill our two bravest and fiercest guards!' the demon at the front said to the others. 'Look at them, they're just lying there!'

And they all began to quiver and quake with fear, and the demons at the back pushed forward to see what it was that had stopped the ones at the front. And when they saw the guards' bodies, they began to quake and quiver too. These demons, you see, like most bullies, weren't actually very brave. They just used their size to frighten people. They all started to get very worried.

And at that moment, the pheasant started flying into their faces and pecking at their noses, and the dog snapped at their ankles, and the monkey began to throw fruit down on to their heads from a tree above.

'Oh no, it's the boy's magic powers at work. Something terrible is happening. We're being attacked from every side!' the demons screamed.

And they ran and ran to the edge of the island, where they got into their ships and sailed away, never to be seen again. And good riddance to them.

After all this, Momo-taro-san and the animals were very tired, so as it was getting dark they decided to look for somewhere to sleep, and go back home the next day. It was almost dark when they found a cave, which looked inviting, and they lay down to sleep. Within a few minutes all the animals were fast asleep, but not Momo-taro-san. He just couldn't get comfortable. The ground seemed so hard, and he tried this position, he tried that position, but it was no use. He couldn't sleep at all. It was as though there were little pebbles digging into him all night. And as soon as it got light, the first

thing he did was to look and see what was on the floor in the cave that was so uncomfortable.

And when he did, he couldn't believe his eyes! Can you guess what he found there? I'll give you a clue; it was something you might be very pleased to find. It was – GOLD! The floor of the cave was covered in pieces of gold. The demons had stolen it from a pirate ship, you see, and put it in the cave as they didn't really know what to do with it.

When Momo-taro-san saw all this gold everywhere, he woke up the animals and shouted, 'Look! Look! Here's gold!'

The animals each opened a sleepy eye, 'Why are you waking us up so early?'

'Look,' he said. 'We're rich!'

They looked down and saw these yellow stones that didn't look very exciting to them, and they turned over and were about to go back to sleep.

Momo-taro-san cried, 'No, come on. Get up. This is gold!'

The dog sniffed it. 'It doesn't smell very nice.' Then he licked it, 'It doesn't taste very nice either. Ow! It nearly broke my tooth when I tried to eat it.'

'You can't eat gold,' said Momo-taro-san. 'We'll all be rich.'

Then the monkey piped up, 'I think this is a trick. We came here because you promised to share out your kibidango, and now you're trying to make us take this yellow stuff instead. If we can't eat it, it's no use to us.'

And then the pheasant had a very good idea. 'Well,' she said, 'if you're so excited by this gold, why don't *you* have it all, and we'll have your share of the kibidango.'

So it was agreed. Momo-taro-san took all the gold he could carry in a bag over his shoulder, and they all went home. When Momo-taro-san's parents found out that they wouldn't have to be poor anymore they were very pleased, but even happier to see their son safe and well.

But, do you know, Momo-taro-san never forgot the animals. Every week he would take a big food parcel down to the forest where they lived, and so for the rest of their days they had as much kibidango as they could eat!

Bhambhutia

Once upon a time there was an old woman who lived with her daughter, Sona, in a little house in a little village. When Sona was about sixteen years of age, her mother decided it was time for her to be married. She found her a nice young man and when they were married, Sona went to live with her husband in another village far away on the other side of the jungle.

The old woman lived on her own in the house now, and after a while she began to feel very lonely. She decided she must go and visit her daughter. But how could she get there? The jungle was full of wild animals and there were no buses or trains to take her.

'I can't even walk properly,' she thought. 'I'm such an old woman.'

She kept thinking and thinking and thinking, and at last she decided that she would take only a few clothes in a small bag so that she wouldn't have much to carry, and she would take a big walking stick to support her. So one bright morning, she set off into the jungle.

Now in the jungle there lived a lion. As the old woman approached him, the lion heard the sound of her walking stick going:

Thabook, thabook, thabook, thabook.

'Who is this coming by making this *thabook thabook* noise?' he asked himself. Then he saw the old woman. And what did the lion say? He said:

Dosima, dosima,

Hoong tune khaun.

This means, 'Old woman, I want to eat you.'
But the old woman replied:

Mari dikari ne,

Ghare java de,

Taji maji thava de,

Puchi mane khaje.

And this means, 'Please let me go to my daughter's house first. I'll get fat and juicy there and then you can eat me when I come back.'

So the lion said, 'Mmm, that sounds like a good idea. But mind you come back soon.'

So the old woman went on her journey.

Further on there lived a tiger, and in the distance he heard:

Thabook, thabook, thabook, thabook.

'Who is this coming by making this *thabook thabook* noise?' he asked himself. Then he saw the old woman coming. And what do you think he said?

Dosima, dosima,
Hoong tune khaun.

That's right. He said, 'Old woman, I want to eat you.'
And what did the old woman reply?

Mare dikare ne,
Ghare java de,
Taji maji thava de,
Puchi mane khaje.

'Please let me go to my daughter's house first. I'll get fat and juicy there, and then you can eat me when I come back.'

And the tiger thought this was a good idea, so he let her go on her way, saying, 'Make sure you come back though!'

A little further on lived a fox and a bear who also heard the sound of the old woman's stick:

Thabook, thabook, thabook, thabook.

'Who is this coming by making this *thabook thabook* noise?' they wondered. And they came out of their cave and met the old woman. And what did they say to her?

Dosima, dosima,
Hoong tune khaun.

'Old woman, we want to eat you.'
And the old woman said:

Mare dikare ne,
Ghare java de,
Taji maji thava de,
Puchi mane khaje.

'Please let me go to my daughter's house first. I'll get fat and juicy there and then you can eat me when I come back.'

And the fox and the bear thought that would be nice so they let the old woman go on her way, saying, 'Make sure you come back though!'

By this time the old woman had come to the edge of the jungle and there before her was a little path leading to her daughter's house. So in she went and stayed with her daughter. And there were lots of things to say, and lots to eat and she lived there very happily.

After a month, she decided it was time to come home, but she was very worried. She told her daughter about the lion, the tiger, the fox and the bear who all wanted to eat her up.

'How can I go back home? They will kill me and eat me. Can you think of anything, Sona?'

'Stay a while longer,' said Sona, 'and we'll think about it.'

So another month passed whilst they both thought about it and the old woman kept on eating and enjoying herself. She was very fat and juicy by this time, in fact she was so fat that she looked completely round like a big round pot – a *bhambhutia*. And one day that gave her an idea.

'I'll become a bhambhutia,' she said. 'Let's make a big clay pot and I'll get inside and you can push it so that it goes roley poley all the way home.'

So they made a great big round clay pot and the old woman squeezed herself into it. Her daughter put the lid on and then pushed it off down the road from the front door.

The bhambhutia went roley poley, roley poley down the road:

Doolook doolook, doolook doolook.

In the distance, the fox and the bear could hear it coming.

'What is this *doolook doolook, doolook, doolook?*' they asked each other.

When they saw the bhambhutia, they ran up to it and stopped it, and asked, 'Hey, *doolook doolook*, have you seen an old woman who went by here about a couple of months ago. We want to eat her. Do you know her at all? Is she coming back?'

Then the old woman replied from inside the bhambhutia:

Kis ki dosi kis ka kaam,

Chal bhambhutia upne gaam.

And this means, 'Which old woman do you want? I don't know anybody. Come on, bhambhutia, let's go on to our own village.'

And on it went:

Doolook doolook, doolook doolook.

But the fox and the bear were curious, so they followed along behind. When they came to the tiger, the tiger stopped the bhambhutia and said, 'Wait a minute, *doolook doolook.* Have you seen an old woman coming. Do you know her name? Is she coming back or not?'

And the old woman replied from inside the bhambhutia:

**Kis ki dosi kis ka kaam,
Chal bhambhutia upne gaam.**

The bhambhutia rolled on again:

Doolook doolook, doolook doolook.

But the tiger was curious too and he followed along behind the bear and the fox.

Further along the road, the lion was sitting waiting for the old woman to come back. When he saw the bhambhutia coming he said, 'Wait, wait, *doolook doolook,* I want to speak to you. Have you seen an old woman? Do you know her name or where she is? Is she coming back or not?'

The old woman replied again:

**Kis ki dosi kis ka kaam,
Chal bhambhutia upne gaam.**

And it started rolling again:

Doolook doolook, doolook doolook.

Roley poley, roley poley it went all the way back to the old woman's front door. But the lion had followed the tiger, the tiger had followed the fox and the bear, and they all sat down to wait and see what would happen next.

The old woman didn't come out. She just stayed in the bhambhutia and waited. At last it got really dark and quiet. The lion, the tiger, the fox and the bear all fell fast asleep one by one.

At midnight the old woman looked out carefully, then out she crawled. Very softly and slowly she said to the bhambhutia:

Teri dosi tera kaam

Jaow bhambhutia upne gaam.

'Bhambhutia, you saved me, and you did so well, I'll let you go wherever you want to live.'

Could the bhambhutia go on on its own? No! So the bhambhutia has stayed outside the old woman's house ever since and keeps the old woman company. And the lion, the tiger, the fox and the bear went back into the jungle and waited and waited for the old woman to come back. Did she come back? No! So they are waiting still in that jungle. And that bhambhutia is still sitting outside a little old house in that little village.

Did the Rum Do?

I don't know is it true or is it a lie. But if it's a lie, it wasn't me that made it up. So you can't call me a liar. Listen here to me.

Once in Ireland, a good while ago, there was a fella and he lived in a snug little house on the side of a woody hill. Now, don't ask me the fella's name, for there's a thing I don't know. But I *do* know this: the fella had three daughters and there wasn't a thing those three girls couldn't do. They could change the wheel on a bicycle; they could fix a rickety chair; they could weave and knit and spin and sew. They could answer any question you could think of. Just about. They were the best three girls in all of Ireland. And that was good and it wasn't bad!

Sometimes they called the fella 'Da', sometimes they called him 'Dad' and sometimes they called him 'Daddy'. But he didn't mind what they called him so long as they were good – which they nearly always were. Wasn't he the lucky man?

Mind you, he was fairly poor. The times were hard and the landlords were greedy; they'd throw you out of house and home if you couldn't pay your rent. But he was alright and so were the girls. They never were hungry and they never were cold. How would they be cold with the woody hill right there beside them? They always had plenty of logs to put on the fire and keep themselves warm. And with eggs from the chickens, and honey from the bees, and milk and cheese and butter from the cow and good things to eat from the garden – they didn't do too badly at all.

But how did they manage in the winter time when the woody hill was covered with snow and nothing would grow in the garden? They saved up food from the spring and the summer – that's what they did. And they were the best times of all because there wasn't much work to be done in the winter and that gave their Daddy a chance to sit down. And then he'd sometimes play them some tunes and then . . . they would *dance*! It would do your heart good to see them and to hear the clatter of their shoes on the kitchen floor. You could hear it a mile down the road, if you happened to be there. Slip-jigs, single-jigs, double-jigs and reels; hornpipes, marches, polkas and slides! And as for the lovely sound of the tin-whistle! I didn't tell you the fella played the tin-whistle did I? Well he did. That's what he'd play the tunes on. And he'd play the tunes, the three girls would dance and everything would be just right. Near enough. They were the best times of all.

But then one night the girls noticed something wrong. Their Daddy said he wouldn't eat his dinner, he just sat down hunched up by the fire with his head in his hands and a face on him as long as today and tomorrow – very miserable and glum.

So the eldest girl, she said, 'What's up with you, Da?'

The fella said this. 'Arrah, girls,' he said, 'girls, I've a terrible . . .!'

Well, that wasn't much of an answer. So the next girl, she said, 'What's up with you, Dad?'

'Arrah, girls,' he said, 'don't be moithering me,' he said. 'Can't you see, I've a terrible . . .!'

Well, they still hadn't a clue what he was talking about.

So the littlest girl, she said, 'What's up with you, Daddy?'

And then he explained. 'Arrah, girls,' he said, 'I've a terrible, rotten dose of a *cold*.

I'm feeling sick and I'm going straight to my bed. There'll be no music and no dancing tonight.'

And off he went to his bed. And that was bad and it wasn't good!

Oh the poor man! Well, you know what it's like when you have a cold: you're coughing and sneezing all the time, you're feeling hot one minute and cold the next and you can't get to sleep. Oh the poor man! And oh the poor girls! They were so disappointed.

'What'll we do?' said the littlest one. 'What'll we do now?'

Well, they hummed and they hawed. They sat on one chair and then on another. They looked out the window and they looked out the door. They put their heads together and they thought very hard.

Then the eldest one said this. 'Listen here to me,' she said, 'and I'll tell you what we'll do: if Daddy is sick, we'll have to make him better. Come on!'

Well, they searched all the cupboards and they searched all the drawers but dear me – not a drop of medicine could they find. They turned the whole place upside down and still they couldn't find any. But do you know what they *did* find? They found a big bottle of rum.

'That'll do, that'll do,' the little one said.

They poured a little drop of rum into a glass. Then they got a lemon and they squeezed the juice of it in with the rum. Then they put some honey and spices in, topped it up with steaming hot water, tiptoed into their Daddy's room and handed him the glass.

'Here, Daddy,' they said, 'drink that.'

He took the glass and he held it up to the light. As it didn't look too bad, he sniffed it. As it didn't smell too bad, he sipped it and, as it didn't taste too bad, he drank it all down. Well, in less time than it takes to tell, he fell fast asleep and the three girls tiptoed out of the room and went to their beds.

'That'll do the trick,' they said. 'That'll surely cure him.'

Next morning, they were up at the crack of dawn to see how their Daddy was. But when they stepped into the kitchen – there he was, sitting hunched up by the fire, looking just as miserable and glum as the night before. Surely all those good things mixed together in the glass had done the trick and cured the cold by now?

The littlest one, she said, 'Did the rum do?'

She was sure it *had* 'done'. So she said it again a bit louder, *'Did the rum do?'*

The fella shook his head and sniffed: 'Sniff!'

So the next one, she said, 'Did the rum do, Da?'

She was sure it had 'done' too. So she said it again a bit louder still, *'Did the rum do, Da?'*

The fella just shook his head again and sniffed: 'Sniff!'

So the eldest one, she said, 'Did the rum do, Daddy?'

Now, she was three times as sure as her sisters. So she said it again even louder, *'Did the rum do, Daddy?'*

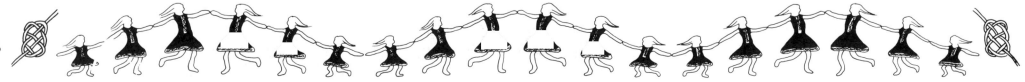

Well, the fella smiled, then he grinned and then he laughed. 'Yes,' he said. 'Yes,' he said, 'the rum *did* do and my cold is gone! I was only tricking you just now. The rum *did* do and I'm feeling *grand*!'

They laughed and they laughed till they were all fit to burst.

Then up piped the littlest one, 'I know what we'll do. We'll make up a tune! And I know what the words will be:'

Did the rum do da do da do da?
Did the rum do da do daddy?

They set to work making up the tune together straight away. They thought of a good one in next to no time and they taught it to their Daddy. It was a hard tune to learn but he got it in the end. Then, of course, he played it on the tin-whistle and up stepped the girls onto the floor. Then began . . . THE DANCING!

Indeed, I saw them all not three weeks ago and they were all still dancing.

Did the rum do da do da do da, Did the rum do da do dad-dy?

Di-the-rum doo da doo da doo da, Di-the-rum doo da, doo da dee. Did-ly

doo did-ly da did-ly doo did-ly dum did-ly doo dee da did-ly di-the-rum dee dum. Did-ly

doo did-ly da did-ly di-the-rum dee da, did-ly

did-ly id-le dum did-ly id-le doo-dle dum, Dee did-ly id-le dum did-ly id-le doo-dle dum.

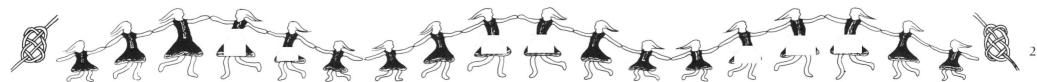

The Night Troll

Once there was a girl who lived on a farm away up in the north of Iceland. The farmsteads were all very isolated: it was a good ride to the nearest neighbour, and it took a full day to get to the local church. Still, every Christmas Eve, everyone would go there, no matter how far it was, for the Christmas service – and for the socializing, gossiping and fun afterwards.

Now the girl belonged to a large family, and there was a baby too, who was much too young for the long ride to the church. But the trouble was, it wasn't safe for anyone to stay behind at the farm on Christmas Eve. There were too many trolls and ogres and ghosts about at that time of year, and this particular farm was really unlucky in any case. If anyone did stay there on that night, they would be found next morning mad or dead. Or sometimes they would just vanish away without a trace.

But this year, anyway, someone *had* to stay because of the baby, and the girl said she would do it, she wasn't scared. She knew all about trolls and such creatures and how to manage them. The thing to do was not to get scared and not to look at them, and above all never to let them get the last word. Trolls love a good argument, especially if it's witty or poetic, and if you can keep them talking till the sun comes up, they'll be turned to stone by the first ray of light. The girl knew this and she was clever and quick, so she wasn't worried. All the people went off to church, and she was left with the baby, Kari. And she was rocking it, and singing it to sleep, calm as you please.

Little Kari, hushaby oh,
Dilly do dilly do.
Little Kari, hushaby oh,
Dilly do dilly do.

ári minn Kari, og korriro,
dillidó og dillidó.
ári minn Kari, og korriro,
dillidó og dillidó.

Lit - tle Ka - ri__ hush-a - bye oh,
á - ri minn Ka-ri, og kor - ri - ro,
ow - ree min Ka-ree, org kaw - ree - ror,

Dil - ly do__ dil - ly do.__
dił - li - dó og dil - li - dó.__
dil - lee - daw org dil - lee - daw.__

Lit - tle Ka - ri,__ hush-a - bye oh,
á - ri minn Ka-ri, og kor- ri - ro,
ow - ree min Ka-ree, org kaw- ree - ror,

Dil - ly do____ dil - ly do.
dil - li - dó__ og dil - li - dó.
dil - lee - daw org dil - lee - daw.

But then all of a sudden she hears the shuffling and stamping of enormous feet, and the whole house starts to shake. And she knows that a troll is coming, but she doesn't look up. She just keeps on rocking the baby and singing away. And by and by she hears a great snorting and snuffling and smacking of lips, and there it is pressed against the window, peering in at her and

close enough to touch! But she still doesn't look up, she just keeps on minding the baby. Then the troll suddenly roars out, like it's singing along with her.

**Look, your eyes are kind and mild,
Look at mine so fierce and wild.**

Look your eyes are_ kind and mild,_

Look at mine so fierce and wild._

But the girl doesn't so much as throw the troll a glance. She just sings back quick as a flash:

**My eyes shine with love and caring,
Yours stare so cruel and glaring.**

My eyes shine with_ love and ca - ring,

Yours stare_ so cruel and gla - ring.

Oh, then the troll starts scratching at the window with its great long nails and it howls out even louder:

**See your hands so soft and dainty,
Look at mine all hard and hairy.**

And again the girl answers it straight back:

**My hands soothe and gently touch,
Yours scratch and snatch and clutch.**

The troll is really angry now, and it's stamping its feet as it sings out even louder:

**See your feet, so small and pretty,
Look at mine, all huge and heavy.**

But the girl just gently taps her feet to the beat as she softly answers it back:

**My feet lightly dance and skip,
Yours trample, stamp and trip.**

Now, the time is passing and dawn is coming. The troll tries one more time:

**Hear your voice so sweet and soothing,
Listen – mine is fierce and roaring.**

But without even pausing for breath, the girl replies like this:

**My voice sends a child to sleep,
Yours makes a grown man weep.**

And at last the troll gives up with the song, and simply bellows to her:
'Look over your shoulder at me, my dear,
I've something lovely for you here.'

'Look over your shoulder yourself,' says she.
'There's something there for you to see.'

And the troll looks round, and what does he see? – the sun rising up behind the mountain. With a terrible shriek, he turned into stone, a huge stone troll just outside the door. And there he has stayed to this very day – so if you don't believe me, you can go there and see for yourself.

Why the Grass Never Stops Growing

This is a story from Western Uganda where everyone speaks Swahili as well as their own local language. So a Swahili greeting goes:

Ham jambo. (Hello.)
Si jambo. (Hello.)
Habari? (How are you?)
Mzuri! (Beautiful!)

Once upon a time there lived a man called Yusufu and his wife Fatima. They had four children: two daughters, Mariama and Amina, and two sons, Dawid and Isaka.

Yusufu and Fatima were coffee farmers. Each year, before the rains came, they would go to their farm every day and work from sunrise to sunset. Yusufu would take a cutlass and work on one part of the farm. Fatima would use a hoe to weed the other side. Sometimes Yusufu would go and inspect Fatima's work to see if the ground had been properly cleared.

Meanwhile, the children would be left in charge of the house. They did the shopping, the cooking, the cleaning, the washing and ironing as well as the washing-up. They even had to go down to the river to fetch water every morning and evening. These four children were very hardworking indeed.

But now one day Yusufu noticed that there was grass all over the area that Fatima had been weeding. Yusufu was not amused. He thought that Fatima hadn't done any work all that time. 'You're a lazy woman,' he said. 'You're not going to work on the farm anymore.'

Fatima was very upset.

'I do get rid of the grass,' she protested, 'but it keeps growing back again.'

The children were also upset because they knew their mother worked harder than anyone. But Yusufu wouldn't listen. Next day Fatima had to stay at home with the children, while Yusufu went to the farm alone. But at noon when Yusufu stopped for a break, he heard a song:

Titi butitira,
Titi butitira,
Karaere, karaere munywanyi wako,
Titi butitira,
Karaere, karaere munywanyi wako.

Ti - ti bu-ti - ti - ra,

Ti - ti bu-ti - ti - ra, Ka -

- rae - re, Ka-rae-re mun-ywan-yiwa-ko,

Ti - ti bu-ti - ti - ra, Ka -

- rae - re, Ka-rae-re mun-ywan-yi wa-ko.

Yusufu followed the singing until he came to a huge, tall tree where a little bird sat high up in the branches singing. He stopped and listened, enjoying the song. Then suddenly, right at the end of the song, the bird called out:

Kasindo, teruk, teruk, teruk!
(Grass, grow, grow, grow!)

And it flew from the tree, spreading its wings and dancing in the air to the song it was singing. Then it landed on the ground and began to pick seeds for its meal.

Kasindo, teruk, teruk, teruk!

And everywhere it went the grass began to grow! Yusufu followed the bird and tried again and again to catch it, but he couldn't.

'How wicked,' he sighed. And he picked up his cutlass and went home to apologise to Fatima.

'You were right,' he said, and he told Fatima and the children all about the little bird.

'Would you come with me tomorrow?' he pleaded with his wife.

'Alright, I'll come,' said Fatima, 'and we'll catch that bird.'

Early the next morning, Yusufu and Fatima set off with a large basket and a pocket full of seeds. They walked quickly and soon reached the farm.

At noon, the little bird began to sing and dance again:

Titi butitira . . .

Then it called:

Kasindo, teruk, teruk, teruk!

Yusufu and Fatima could see it sitting high up in the tree. It was safe out of reach. But it was a very greedy bird. As soon as Yusufu scattered the seeds, it flew down to the ground. It picked up every single seed and swallowed it. Soon it was too heavy to fly back up into the tree.

Fatima went quickly behind the bird and placed the basket over it. 'Hooray,' she shouted, 'the bird is trapped!'

Yusufu tilted the basket a little, and put his hand underneath it to get hold of the bird. He thought to himself, 'I've a good mind to squash you, little bird.' . . . But Yusufu was a kind-hearted man. He wouldn't have hurt a fly.

So Yusufu and Fatima took the bird home. They showed it to their children and explained why it had been trapped. Then Yusufu put the bird underneath a large basket with some food and water. Finally, he placed a heavy stone on the top of the basket.

'There!' he said. 'The bird is caught, and now the grass will stop growing.'

And he warned the children never never to let the bird out.

The following morning, Yusufu and Fatima went back to work on the farm. But while they were away the children kept thinking about the bird. Finally their curiosity got the better of them, and they lifted the basket to have a peep. And without hesitation, of course, the little bird flew away.

When Yusufu and Fatima returned home, they knew, without anyone having to tell them, that the bird had escaped. 'Children, oh children!' Yusufu cried. 'Do you know what you have done? Now the grass will grow again. You have given us more work to do. But you have also given work to yourselves, your future children, your children's children and generations to come.

As far as I know, the greedy little bird is still free to this day. It is still calling out to the grass to grow. That is why the grass never stops growing.

Ojame? (Brother?)
E? (Yes?)
Iwachoni? (Are you still there?)
Ehe! (I sure am!)

Kibungo

The Amazon rainforest is the biggest forest in the world. The tall, tall trees grow close together and their branches make a green roof that shuts out the sky. Inside it is dark and dangerous and full of life – spiders and snakes, colourful birds, jaguars, armadillos, chattering monkeys and bright lizards. The Amerindian people, who have always lived there, know all these creatures, and tell stories about them. Here is a song about one of them:

Kibungo oi bicho do mato,
Kibungo oi bicho do mato.
(*Repeat ad lib.*)

(Kibungo, beast of the forest.)

Ki - bun - go   oi   bi - cho do   ma - to.   Ki - bun - go
Kee-boon - go   oi   bee - shoo doo   ma - too.   Kee-boon - go

End   *Repeat ad lib.*

oi   bi - cho   do   mato.   Ki - bun - go
oi   bee - shoo   doo   mat.   Kee - boon - go

Do you know who Kibungo is? He is a horrible hairy creature, a monster. He is eight feet tall, with four arms and one eye, and three mouths full of pointed teeth. And he smells! Eurgh! Kibungo smells terrible!

Do you know what he eats? Anything and everything. He'd eat you if he could. He'd catch you and take you back to his small cave full of bones. Scrunch! Scrunch! And Kibungo is always hungry. So now you know why everyone in the forest keeps away from Kibungo.

Well, on this particular morning Kibungo woke up feeling very, very hungry. 'Today I want a big big meal,' he said to himself. 'Today I want a feast! I don't want one animal. I don't want two. I want to catch all the animals in the forest, and eat every one!'

So he took a big sack and hurried down to the waterhole, where the animals came to drink every morning. He hid behind a bush and waited.

First to arrive was the jaguar. Slowly and carefully she padded down to the water and began to drink, 'Clop clop clop.'

Kibungo crept out, quietly, quietly, and grabbed her from behind. And into the sack she went. Grawwawwa!

Next came the snake, sliding lazily down to the water to drink, 'Sssep sssep sssep.'

Up jumped Kibungo and grabbed her by the neck. And into the sack she went. Hsst.

The monkey was next and Kibungo grabbed him by the tail. Next came the armadillo and he was caught too. And so it went on, all morning, until the sack was full and no more animals came to drink.

'I must have caught them all,' thought Kibungo.

So he set off home, feeling very pleased with himself, dragging the sack behind him. Bump bump bump went the sack, and the animals howled and hissed but they

couldn't get out. Through the forest they went, until they came to a clearing. And right in the middle of the clearing, on a nice sunny rock, was Jabuti the tortoise. Kibungo stopped and stared at Jabuti, and his mouth watered, because tortoise is very, very tasty. And Jabuti stared at Kibungo and his big bag and her mouth went dry with fear, because she knew how greedy Kibungo was. It was no good trying to run away, because a tortoise is very slow as you know.

But Jabuti was very, very clever, and she thought very hard and very fast until she thought of a plan.

'Kibungo!' she cried. 'How wonderful to see you! You're the very one I wanted to see.'

Kibungo never thought Jabuti would be pleased to see him! But there she was, dancing up and down and waving her flute in the air. Now Jabuti's flute was a magic flute made of deer bone. She could play every kind of song.

'Kibungo!' she cried. 'I've got a new tune. A magic dancing tune. Only a really good dancer can do it. But *you* are a really good dancer, Kibungo. The best dancer in the whole forest. Would you like to try?'

'No,' said Kibungo. 'I'm hungry.'

'Oh, please!' begged Jabuti. 'You are so graceful, so agile.'

'Well . . .' said Kibungo.

'So splendid! So handsome!' cried Jabuti.

'But . . .' said Kibungo.

'So elegant! So lovable,' added Jabuti.

Well, no one had ever called Kibungo handsome before and no one had ever, ever called him lovable. He began to feel even more pleased with himself.

'Oh very well!' he said. 'I will dance this dance for you, because I am such a wonderful dancer. But after that, I'll eat you! So no tricks!'

'Of course not,' said Jabuti, and she began to play the flute. It was a lovely tune. It made you want to dance:

FLUTE, RECORDER, VOICE *(sing to la)*

'Hurry up,' said Kibungo. 'What do I do?'

'It's the dance of the spinning top, and it has a song too. The song tells you what to do,' said Jabuti. 'So first you have to step round in a circle, holding your arms out like a top.'

'Easy!' said Kibungo, and he stamped about clumsily:

(Verse 1)
O pião entrou na roda ó pião,
O pião entrou na roda ó pião.

'Now the chorus,' said Jabuti. 'Spin round, and rock from side to side.'

'No problem!' said Kibungo, whirling and whirling:

(*Chorus*)
Roda ó pião, bambeia pião,
Roda ó pião, bambeia pião.

'Now do a tap dance!' said Jabuti. 'And spin round again:'

(*Verse 2 and chorus*)
Sapateia no terreiro ó pião,
Sapateia no terreiro ó pião.
   Roda ó pião, bambeia pião,
   Roda ó pião, bambeia pião.

'Lovely! Lovely!' said Jabuti. 'And now …'

And then all of a sudden Jabuti stopped, and took the flute out of her mouth.

'Oh dear!' she said. 'Oh, Kibungo. I'm sorry, Kibungo, but you can't do this dance after all!'

'What?' shouted Kibungo. 'Can't do it? After I have been dancing so beautifully? Of course I can do it!'

'But you see,' said Jabuti, 'the next verse says take the hand of your partner. And you haven't got anyone to dance with, Kibungo. So you can't do it.'

Kibungo screamed and stamped and snarled and wailed. But it was no good. He couldn't do the dance without a partner. Then suddenly he remembered his sack full of animals. Of course! He could dance with one of them! He opened the sack and pulled out the monkey.

'Splendid!' said Jabuti. 'Now you are ready. Hold right hands and circle one way, swap hands and circle the other way. One, two, three and off you go!'

And off went Kibungo and the monkey whirling and twirling through the dance:

(*Verse 3 and chorus*)
Pega a mão do teo parceiro ó pião,
Pega a mão do teo parceiro ó pião.
   Roda ó pião, bambeia pião,
   Roda ó pião, bambeia pião.

'Now choose a new partner,' said Jabuti, and Kibungo dived for his sack. He was so busy dancing he didn't notice the monkey, sneaking off into the jungle as fast as he could.

And so Kibungo danced with one animal after another, and as soon as the animals finished dancing with him they each slipped away quietly. On and on and on they danced, until at last Kibungo looked in the sack for a new partner and there were no animals left. He stopped dancing and looked around, but everyone had gone, except for Jabuti who was still playing the flute.

When Kibungo realised that he had been tricked he was furious! He jumped at Jabuti gnashing his teeth. But his legs were so tired after all that dancing, they just gave way under him, and he fell panting on to the floor. And there he had to stay, until he got enough strength back to crawl home, very hungry, very, very tired, and very, very, very angry.

But as for Jabuti, she smiled to herself, picked up her flute and went on down to the waterhole singing to herself:

O pião entrou na roda ó pião . . .

The Strange Visitor

There was an old woman who lived on her own,
And all alone was she,
And no one around for miles and miles
To keep her company.

One night she sat beside the fire
A-spinning at the wheel,
But as she sat she said, said she,
'How lonely I do feel!'

**And still she sat and still she span,
And still she wished for company.**

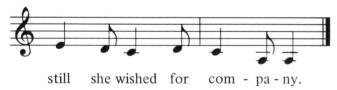

Then in came a pair of great big feet –

 (*drum*)

And set themselves down in front of the fire.

**And still she sat and still she span,
And still she wished for company.**

Then in came a pair of thin, thin legs –

(*woodblock*)

And settled themselves on top of the feet.

**And still she sat and still she span,
And still she wished for company.**

Then in came a great big muscley body –

(*drum*)

And set itself down on top of the legs.

**And still she sat and still she span,
And still she wished for company.**

Then in came a thin, thin pair of arms –

(*woodblock*)

And set themselves down on top of the body.

**And still she sat and still she span,
And still she wished for company.**

Then in came a great big pair of hands –

(*drum*)

And they fixed themselves on to the end of the arms.

**And still she sat and still she span,
And still she wished for company.**

Then in came a thin, thin skinny neck –

(*woodblock*)

And it set itself down on top of the body.

**And still she sat and still she span,
And still she wished for company.**

Then in came a great big, horrible head –

(*drum*)

And it set itself down on top of the neck.

**And still she sat and still she span,
And still she wished for company.**

Old Woman:
'But why have you got such great big feet?'

Strange Visitor:
'From walking far, from walking far.'

'Then why have you got such wee thin legs?'

'From staying up late and little food.'

'Then why have you got such a great big body?'

'From carrying things, from carrying things.'

'Then why have you got such wee thin arms?'

'From staying up late and little food.'

'Then why have you got such great big hands?'

'From working hard, from working hard.'

'Then why have you got such a wee thin neck?'

'From staying up late and little food.'

'And why have you got such a great big head?'

'From knowing so much, from knowing so much.'

'And . . . why have you come here?'

'For _____ YOU!'

But up she jumped and grabbed a stick,
And beat it out the door.

Then down she sat and on she span,
And still she wished for company.

And still she sat and still she span,
And still she wished for company.

The Raja's Secret

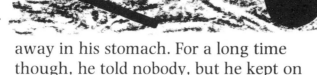

Once upon a time, there was a Raja who had very big ears. He always wore a *kantopi* to hide them. 'If I don't wear a kantopi,' he thought, 'my people will laugh at me, they'll make a joke of my big ears.'

The people didn't know why the Raja always wore a kantopi.

'He's a good Raja,' they said. 'But it's strange, he always wears a kantopi. I wonder why?'

One person said, 'If Raja is wearing one, then I'll wear one too!'

Another said, 'If it's good for Raja, it's good for me too!'

Soon everyone in the kingdom was copying the Raja and wearing a kantopi.

Now the Raja had a royal barber called Manji. Because he cut the Raja's hair, Manji knew the secret of the Raja's big ears.

The Raja had warned Manji, 'You must never tell anyone about my ears. If you do, I shall punish you.'

'I promise you, Your Majesty,' said Manji, 'I will never tell anybody. I will always keep your secret.'

Now Manji had never been able to keep a secret, and this one boiled and bubbled away in his stomach. For a long time though, he told nobody, but he kept on thinking about the Raja's big ears.

One day Manji went into the jungle. 'I wish I could tell someone the Raja's secret,' he groaned.

Suddenly he thought of the answer – he would tell the secret to a tree. Trees don't talk and the secret would be safe. So he found a big, tall tree, sat in front of it and said, 'O tree, listen, I must tell you this.' Then he whispered, *'Our Raja has big ears and to hide them he wears a kantopi all the time. Please keep this to yourself or I'll be punished.'*

After that Manji felt much happier. He went home and forgot about the Raja's secret.

A few days later, a woodcutter was working in the jungle. He saw the fine tall tree.

'Aha, what a big tree,' he thought. 'I'll chop it down and sell the wood.'

He chopped down the tree and cut it into logs and sold them to a factory for good money. Now in the factory they happened to make beautiful musical instruments – flutes, tablas, sitars and tambourines. And what do you think happened next? The instruments which were made from the wood of Manji's tree, were sold to the Royal Musician.

One day, the Raja decided to have a royal party because it was his birthday. The Raja invited many important people from all over his kingdom. At the party everybody was very happy. They ate, talked and laughed together, then after the feast, the Raja called his Royal Musician to him.

'Let us hear our new instruments,' he said. 'Play some happy tunes.'

The music began and everyone was enchanted by it, it was so lovely. But suddenly the Raja leaned forward and looked surprised. To everyone's astonishment the flute was singing away:

**Rajana mota kan, Rajana mota kan,
Rajana mota kan, Rajana mota kan.**

(The Raja has big ears.)

And then the tabla began to beat:

**Tune kone kidhoo, tune kone kidhoo,
Tune kone kidhoo, tune kone kidhoo.**

(Who told you?)

And then the sitar and the tinkling
tambourine replied:

**Umne Manjie kidhoo, umne Manjie kidhoo,
Umne Manjie kidhoo, umne Manjie kidhoo.**

(Manji told us.)

The secret was out. Everyone became very quiet. The Raja's face turned red with anger and shame.

'Bring Manji to the palace at once!' he shouted.

The guards rushed off. When they brought back Manji, he was trembling and shivering with fear. He bowed very low to the Raja and humbly said, 'Your M-M-Majesty, I k-kept your s-s-secret. I only t-told it to a t-tree in the jungle. P-please forgive me.'

Soon the whole story was out. Manji had talked to the tree. The tree had been cut down and sold to the factory. And the musical instruments which had been made from the wood had been bought by the Royal Musician for the Raja's party.

The Raja roared with laughter. 'How stupid I've been!' he said. 'Some people have big ears and some have small. What does it matter? My people love me. I am still clever and I care about my people.'

The Raja forgave Manji and threw away his kantopi. Everyone cheered. They clapped and laughed and threw their kantopis in the air.

The royal band began to play again and everybody danced and sang:

Ek huto Raja,
Ena mota kan.
Vah bhai vah, vah bhai vah,
Vah bhai vah, vah bhai vah.
(Repeat)

(Once there was a Raja,
Raja had big ears.
Shout hurrah! Shout hurrah!
Shout hurrah! Shout hurrah!
(Repeat)

Ek hu – to Ra – ja, E – na mo – ta kan.

Vah bhai vah, vah bhai vah, Vah bhai vah, vah bhai vah.

Ek hu – to Ra – ja, E – na mo – ta kan

Vah bhai vah, vah bhai vah, Vah bhai vah, vah bhai vah.

Colin's Cattle

There was a young man called Colin, who had a little farm with a few cows. He was in love with a girl who was a maid on a nearby farm, and when they were together they were happy as could be. They used to walk across the moors, hand in hand, singing and laughing. But they didn't have much time, because mostly they had to work, you see, starting from half past four in the morning. She had to milk the cows and clean the big ranges and work for the people on her farm, and he had his cows and his farm to see to. Whenever she could, she'd come and help him, especially with milking the cows.

So that was alright. But then the fairies got jealous – they resent anyone being too happy. So one day the girl fell asleep out on the moors and the fairies came and took her, and whished her off to fairyland. And they wouldn't let her go back to Colin. They thought maybe he'd forget her and that would be the end of it. But the girl was worried that Colin wouldn't manage things alone and she begged and pleaded to be allowed to go and help him with his cows at least. And the fairies gave in, and

said she could go and milk Colin's cows every morning. But to make sure he wouldn't see her – they made her invisible.

The girl didn't complain or object, she just agreed. And so the next day, she got up very early and went off to Colin's farm, and she was invisible, just like the fairies said: no one could see her. But now, when she started to milk the cows, do you know what she did? She started to sing to them, like this:

Mine ain Colin's cattle,
Dapple brown, dun and grey,
I return for to milk them
At the break of the day.

So she sang and she sang. And Colin heard a voice coming from the cowshed. He went in, and he looked about, and there were the cows all lined up to be milked but he couldn't see anybody there. But he could hear! and when he heard the voice, of course he recognised it. He knew it was the voice of the woman he loved.

So the very next day, at the very same time, he went back to the shed, and he waited. And sure enough the cows lined up to be milked, though he couldn't see who was doing it. And then, once again he heard the song:

Mine ain Colin's cattle,
Dapple brown, dun and grey,
I return for to milk them
At the break of the day.

Well then, one thing at least was clear to Colin. She was there, even if he couldn't see her, and she hadn't gone off altogether and left him. And if she was invisible, and being held against her will, it must be something to do with the fairies somehow. But at least it seemed he could hear her, and be near her sometimes, and that was better than nothing at all.

So day after day, week after week, year after year he used to go into the cattleshed, and listen while she was milking. And of course, then, he didn't forget her even though he could not see her. So this went on for seven years, and at the end of that time the fairies had to give up. They saw they were never going to separate those two, or spoil that love.

So they gave up, and they gave in with a good grace too. They let the girl go back to him, visible, and well as ever and to make up for that seven years, they gave two wishes, one for her and one for him. Do you know what they wished for? Why, wealth and health of course, and with that they lived happily ever after.

The Lion on the Path

Once upon a time there was a man and his wife and they were working together in their fields. And the wife she turned to her husband and said, 'Please,' she said, 'I want to go and see my mother.'

And he said, 'What! Again?'

'Yes,' she said, 'it's very important.'

'All right,' he said, 'you go. But when you go, don't you take the big path that goes down the valley. There are lions there. You take the little path that goes up over the hills that all the people take.'

So she said she would. Then she picked up her child and slung him onto her back, put her pot on top of her head and off she went.

Well, she hadn't been gone more than – oh, a very short while – when he said to himself, 'I do believe my wife is on the wrong path. Sure of it!'

So he threw down his hoe, went off to his hut, picked up his little instrument of music, his mbira, (you know, the little one he plays between his hands), and off he went down the path. Now when he got to the place where the two paths divided, there – on the wrong path – were the footprints of his wife! And he said to himself,

'Just like my wife!'

On he went as quickly as he could, down the valley, round behind some trees, and there – standing stock still in the middle of the path – there was his wife; and beyond her, about to spring, was a lion. What could he do? What *could* he do, except to play his instrument of music? So, quickly, he began to play:

Ndongoridza mbira dzangu,
Ndongoridza mbira dzangu.
Ndingadzo fatseketera,
Tseketera na mbira.
  Ti ndi ndi, ti ndi ndi, ti ndi ndi,
  Gore iye, gore wo iye,
  Ti ndi ndi, ti ndi ndi,
  Gore iye, gore wo iye,
  Ti ndi ndi, ti ndi ndi.

(I will play my mbira, thus and thus I'll entertain him with my notes, ti ndi ndi, etc)

And the lion, hearing this most magnificent music, quite forgot about his dinner and began to dance. Then the man quickly pulled his wife round behind him and went on playing.

Now, of course, the man wanted to get away from the lion; but do you know what happened? Every time he took a step back, the lion couldn't hear the music and took a step forward. Now this went on for a very long time and the man was getting more and more tired. (*In a tired and desperate voice:*)

Ndongoridza mbira dzangu . . .

And just when he felt he was altogether exhausted and he couldn't go on playing any longer, a little voice beside him whispered, 'Hey!'

He looked down, and there was – what do you think? – a rabbit!

And Rabbit said, 'Ss-siss! Hand it down to me!'

So without stopping playing for a moment, the man handed his instrument down to Rabbit, and he put up his paws and he went on playing. (*In a high squeaky voice:*)

Ndongoridza mbira dzangu,
Daka daka dai dai za-nza-nza!

(I will play my notes, I will play Daka daka dai dai dai za-nza-nza!)

Man's song with mbira (piano) accompaniment throughout

Ndon-go-rid-zam-bi-rad - zan-gu, Ndon-go-rid-zam-bi - rad - zan-gu

Ndin-gad-zo - fat - se - ke - te - ra, Tse - ke - te - ra nam - bi - ra, Tin-

-din - di, tin - din - di, tin - din - di, Go - re i - ye, go-

-re wo i - ye Tin - din - di, tin - din - di, Go - re i - ye, go-

-re wo i - ye Tin - din - di, tin - din - di.

Rabbit's song

Ndon-go-rid-zam-bi - rad - zan-gu da - ka da - ka da - i da - i da - i zan-zan-za.

Piano (Mbira)

End

GUITAR C   Em   G   Em   C   Em   Am

And Rabbit, he said to the man and his wife, 'Wh-ew! Off you go.'

So, quickly, they went off together, back along the path, towards their home; and Rabbit watched them go until they were safely out of sight, and then, he looked for a place to escape.

There, away on one side, he saw a hole in the ground. And he said to himself, 'That'll do.'

So quickly, he threw down the instrument and bolted down the hole. Well, of course, the moment the magical music stopped, the lion woke up. And all he could see was a rabbit disappearing down a hole.

And he said to himself, 'Bless me!' he said, 'I could have been sure that was a man playing.'

And that was the end of that story.

Toad and Donkey

One day, Bra Toad and Bra Donkey got to arguing about who was the fastest runner. Hear Donkey now: 'I have long tail, and long ear, and a very tall foot, too. I run so fast, fast like a racehorse. And you, you just a too small Toad. How can you race me?'

But Toad just said, 'Hold your noise, Bra Donkey. We'll see about all that.'

So they went to the King to settle it for them. And the King set up a race, a twenty mile race, for Toad and Donkey. And he made a rule that they should shout out after each mile, so everyone could hear how far they'd got.

Now Donkey was all set to go right away, but that smart little Toad fella, he was up to some trick. And he begged and pleaded for a little time to 'fix up his business'. So the King said the race wouldn't start until the next day. Donkey wasn't pleased at all, because he knew Toad was up to something. But the King wouldn't listen, so there was nothing Bra Donkey could do.

Now Toad had twenty picny, twenty children, and they all looked just the same, the dead stamp of each other. So while Bra Donkey was sleeping, Bra Toad took his twenty picny to the race course and he put one down at each mile post. And he said to them all: 'Picny! Hear me now. When that fella Bra Donkey, that jackass, comes down the road shouting and bawling, you just jump up and bawl out, too.'

So all of Toad picny-children settled down to wait by the mile posts. And the race began.

Donkey was so sure he was going to win, he said to himself, 'Cho! No problem! That little bitta fella Toad can't run. Ha! Ha! I'll rest myself and take it easy.'

So he stood about and chewed grass and poked his head through the fences to get a bite of potato and a taste of gungo peas. And he took more than an hour to get to the first mile post.

As he got close, he bawled out:

'Ha! Ha! Ha! Me more than Toad.'

Ha! Ha! Ha! Me more than Toad.

And then up jumped the first picny and called out:

'Jin-ko-ro-ro, jin-kok-kok-kok.'

Jin - ko - ro - ro, jin - kok-kok - kok.

And Donkey was quite surprised and said, 'Tche! How did he come to be before me?' And he thought, 'Maybe I rest myself just too much then. I must go quicker next mile.'

And he set off a bit faster, and only stopped a minute for a drink of water. And as he got to the next post he bawled out:

'Ha! Ha! Ha! Me more than Toad.'

Then the second picny bawled out too:

'Jin-ko-ro-ro, jin-kok-kok-kok.'

An' Donkey say, 'Lah! That little Toad can really move! But no problem I'll beat him this time.'

So he started, an' when he reached the third mile post he bawled out again:

'Ha! Ha! Ha! Me more than Toad.'

And this time it was the third picny who called out from behind the post:

'Jin-ko-ro-ro, jin-kok-kok-kok.'

Donkey was so angry and vexed when he heard Toad answer him again he tried to mash Toad with his foot. But the Toad picny hid himself in the grass. Donkey thought the little fella had gone off ahead, and he nearly bust himself to beat him to the next mile post. He took his tail and used it like a horse-whip and began to gallop. And when he got to the fourth mile post, he was so tired he could barely find breath to call out:

'Ha! Ha! Ha! Me more than Toad.'

But back came the answer once again:

'Jin-ko-ro-ro, jin-kok-kok-kok.'

When Donkey heard him, he started to tremble. 'Lord, what will I do? I must beat that fella.'

And he galloped faster than ever, and harder still. But it was always the same story. Each mile post he got to, he called and the answer came back: 'Jinkororo, jinkokkokkok.'

And Donkey was so shamed that he hung his head, for he saw that he'd lost the race. And Toad, that little bit fella, he won. Because Toad is a trickified thing.

Jack mandora me no choose none.

All Skin and Bone

Now listen carefully to me,
  Hoo hoo hoo hoo! Ha ha ha ha!

Hoo hoo hoo hoo! Ha ha ha ha!

Here's a really ghostly story!
  Hoo hoo hoo hoo! Ha ha ha ha!

There was an old woman all skin and bone,
  Hoo hoo hoo hoo! Ha ha ha ha!
Lived in a little house all alone.
  Hoo hoo hoo hoo! Ha ha ha ha!

Late one night when all was still,
  Hoo hoo hoo hoo! Ha ha ha ha!
She went to the churchyard up the hill.
  Hoo hoo hoo hoo! Ha ha ha ha!

She heard a ghostly sort of moan,
  Hoo hoo hoo hoo! Ha ha ha ha!
Looked right around but she was alone.
  Hoo hoo hoo hoo! Ha ha ha ha!

She creaked open the church door,
  Hoo hoo hoo hoo! Ha ha ha ha!
She'd never been in there before.
  Hoo hoo hoo hoo! Ha ha ha ha!

She saw a coffin long and thin,
  Hoo hoo hoo hoo! Ha ha ha ha!
Opened the lid and peeped right in.
  Hoo hoo hoo hoo! Ha ha ha ha!

Out jumped a ghostie all in white,
  Hoo hoo hoo hoo! Ha ha ha ha!
Gave the old woman a terrible fright.
  Hoo hoo hoo hoo! Ha ha ha ha!

Woman to the ghost did say,
  Hoo hoo hoo hoo! Ha ha ha ha!
'Will I look like you one day?'
  Hoo hoo hoo hoo! Ha ha ha ha!

Ghostie gave a ghastly laugh,
  Hoo hoo hoo hoo! Ha ha ha ha!
'You'll see one day soon enough.'
  Hoo hoo hoo hoo! Ha ha ha ha!

Woman said, 'Oh please tell me,'
  Hoo hoo hoo hoo! Ha ha ha ha!
'When and where that day will be.'
  Hoo hoo hoo hoo! Ha ha ha ha!

Ghost came close and whispered low,
  Hoo hoo hoo hoo! Ha ha ha ha!
'Hoo hoo hoo hoo! Here and NOW!'

Little Cock Featherfrock

Long ago and far away there was a little house in a deep dark forest by a tall steep mountain. In that house lived three friends – a cat, a blackbird, and a little red cock called Petenka or Peetya for short – and on the mountain lived a wicked fox.

The cat looked after the blackbird, the blackbird looked after the cat, and they both looked after Petenka the cock. Whenever the cat and the blackbird went out, they said to him, 'Lock the door and close the windows, and sit on the stove and eat your kalaches. And if the wicked fox comes by, *don't* let him in.'

One day when the cat and the blackbird were out, the fox *did* come. The door was locked, the windows shut, and the little red cock was safe inside sitting warm and snug on the stove.

But the fox stood by the window and sang:

Little Cock Featherfrock,
With your golden comb so red,
And your lovely glossy head,
And your little silky beard,
Look out of the window, please,
And I will give you some peas.

Peetya, Peetya, pitooshok,
Zalatoy gribishok,
Masslina galovooshka,
Sholkava barodooshka,
Vygleenee v akoshechka
Dam tibye garoshichka.

Silly Petenka looked out of the window greedily and the wicked fox grabbed him and put him in a sack. Off he ran towards the mountain, quick, quick, quick. The poor little cock cried with all his might:

The fox is taking me
Beyond the forests deep,
Beyond the river wide,
And up the mountains steep,
Oh save me, Sister Cat!
Oh save me, Sister Cat!

Nissyot minya lissa
Za dreemoochiye lissa,
Za shirokeeye ryekee,
Za tyomneeye goree,
Vasska-cot spassee meenya!
Vasska-cot spassee meenya!

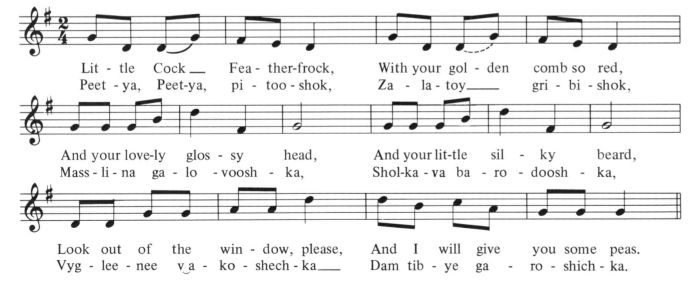

Lit - tle   Cock ___   Fea - ther-frock,   With your gol - den   comb so red,
Peet - ya,   Peet-ya,   pi - too - shok,   Za - la - toy ___   gri - bi - shok,

And your love-ly   glos - sy   head,   And your lit-tle   sil - ky   beard,
Mass - li - na   ga - lo - voosh - ka,   Shol-ka - va   ba - ro - doosh - ka,

Look out   of   the   win - dow, please,   And I   will   give   you some peas.
Vyg - lee - nee   v a - ko - shech - ka ___   Dam tib - ye   ga - ro - shich - ka.

The fox is tak - ing me____ Be - yond the fo - rests deep,____ Be-
Niss - yot min - ya lis - sa____ Za dree-moo - chi - ye lis - sa,____ Za shi -

— yond the ri - ver wide,____ And up the moun - tain steep,____ Oh
— ro — kee - ye rye - kee, Za tyom — nee - ye go — ree, Vass-ka -

save me, Sis - ter Cat!____ Oh save me, Sis - ter Cat!____
— cot spas-see meen - ya!____ Vass-ka - cot spas-see meen - ya!____

Then the cat and the blackbird, who were not so far away, came running to his rescue and chased away the wicked fox.

Now, the next day, the cat and the blackbird were going further away, so they said to Petenka, 'Lock the door, and close the windows, sit on the stove and eat your kalaches. And if the wicked fox comes, remember, *don't let him in!*'

As soon as they were gone, the fox came along. The door was locked, the windows shut, and the little red cock was safe inside, sitting warm and snug on the stove.

So the fox sat down outside the window and sang:

Little Cock Featherfrock . . .

Peetya, Peetya, pitooshok . . .

But this time Petenka sat still and quiet. So then the fox sang even more sweetly:

Boys and girls have passed today,
And scattered corn along the way,
Hens are eating it in flocks,
Giving none to little cocks.

Parnee dyefkee prayeezhalee,
Eepsheneetzoo razbrassalee,
Yeeyo coorachkee sklyooyoot,
Peetooshkoo nee dadoot.

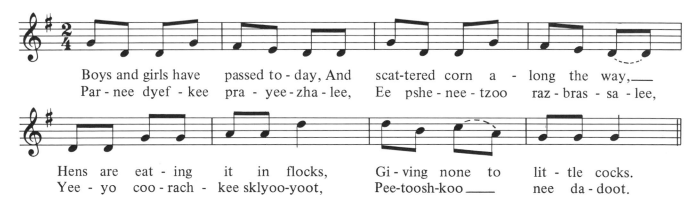

Boys and girls have passed to - day, And scat-tered corn a - long the way,____
Par - nee dyef - kee pra - yee - zha - lee, Ee pshe - nee - tzoo raz - bras - sa - lee,

Hens are eat - ing it in flocks, Gi - ving none to lit - tle cocks.
Yee - yo coo - rach - kee sklyoo-yoot, Pee-toosh-koo____ nee da - doot.

'Why won't they give any to little cocks?' asked Petenka.

And he looked out of the window to see for himself. Quick as a flash, the fox grabbed him, put him in a sack, and ran off towards the mountains.

The poor cock cried with all his might:

The fox is taking me . . .

Nissyot minya lissa . . .

But the cat and the blackbird were too far away to hear, and Petenka cried again with all his strength:

THE FOX IS TAKING ME . . .

NISSYOT MINYA LISSA . . .

This time the cat and the blackbird heard him calling and came running to save him and chase the fox away.

Now, the next day, the cat and the blackbird were going even further away, so they said to the little red cock, 'Lock the door and close the windows, sit on the stove and eat your kalaches. And if the wicked fox comes, remember! DON'T let

him in, and DON'T look out of the window!'

As soon as they were gone, the fox came along. The door was locked, the windows shut, and the little red cock was safe inside, sitting warm and snug on the stove.

So the fox sat down outside the window again and sang:

Little Cock Featherfrock . . .

Peetya, Peetya, pitooshok . . .

Now Petenka listened but he didn't open the window. So then the fox sang even more sweetly:

Boys and girls have passed today . . .

Parnee dyefkee prayeeshalee . . .

Petenka listened even harder, but he still didn't open the window. So then the fox sang even more sweetly still:

Lords and ladies passed today,
And scattered nuts along the way.
Hens are gobbling them up too,
There won't be any left for you.'

Tootbayaree prayeezhalee,
Ee aryeshkee razbrassalee,
Fsye-eeh coorachkee sklyooyoot,
Peetooshkoo nee dadoot.

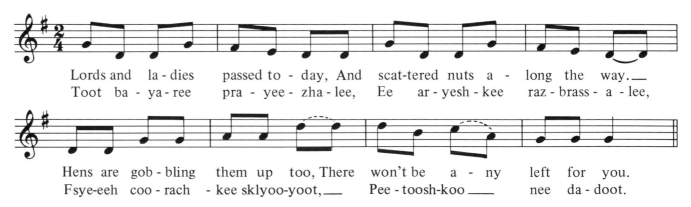

Lords and la - dies   passed to - day, And scat-tered nuts a - long the way.＿
Toot ba - ya - ree   pra - yee - zha - lee,   Ee   ar - yesh - kee   raz - brass - a - lee,

Hens are gob - bling   them up too, There   won't be   a - ny   left for you.
Fsye-eeh coo - rach - kee sklyoo-yoot,＿   Pee - toosh-koo ＿   nee da - doot.

Now Petenka loved nuts even more than corn, so he opened the window to look for himself. Quick as a flash, the fox grabbed him and put him in his sack. Then off he ran faster than fast towards the mountains.

Poor Petenka cried again with all his might:

The fox is taking me . . .

Nissyot minya lissa . . .

He cried again and again, but this time the cat and the blackbird were too far away and they did not hear him.

When at last they came back home, the window was open and the little cock was gone. But on the ground was a trail of fox paw prints. The cat ran and the blackbird flew, following the trail as fast as they could. Through the dark forest, across the wide river, and up the steep mountain, all the way to the fox's lair.

But the door was locked, the entrance blocked, and the fox had the little cock trapped deep inside. So the cat took out her bandoura, and began to sing very sweetly, while the blackbird chirrupped along with the tune:

Listen to us, Foxy-dear,
Are you in your cosy lair?
Your sisters have come visiting,
Foxy, are you there?

Ty seesstreetza lissa,
Vyhadee eez nary,
Tvoee syostry preeshlee,
Vyhadee dye zhe ty.

Petenka heard them singing and so did the wicked fox.

'Sisters?' thought the fox. 'But I don't have any sisters! I wonder who could be singing so nicely out there.'

So he went out to look. And as he stepped outside the blackbird flew up into his face and the cat sprang at him from the side, and Petenka came up from behind and pecked his tail.

And when they had done, the fox felt so sore that he decided he had had enough. He gave up trying to catch Little Cock Featherfrock. So Petenka, the cat and the blackbird went home safely.

And there they live quietly to this very day, munching their bread and sipping their soup.

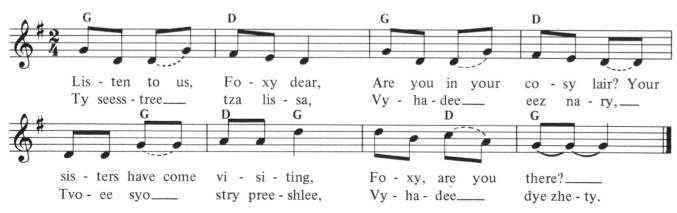

Lis - ten to us, Fo - xy dear, Are you in your co - sy lair? Your
Ty seess-tree___ tza lis-sa, Vy - ha-dee___ eez na - ry,___

sis - ters have come vi - si - ting, Fo - xy, are you there?___
Tvo - ee syo___ stry pree - shlee, Vy - ha-dee___ dye zhe - ty.

The Little Bird and the Raja

Once upon a time in a nest by the river there lived a beautiful little bird. On the other side of the river was a field full of delicious millet and every day birds used to come and feast on it. Now, the man who owned the field of millet was also a birdcatcher, and he was so angry about the birds stealing his millet that he decided to try to catch them. So one evening he spread a net over the field, and next morning he came back to see what he had caught. There, all tangled up in the net, was the beautiful little bird.

When the man saw how beautiful the bird was, he decided to take her and give her to the Raja. He knew if the Raja was pleased, he would give him a rich reward. So he grabbed the bird and put her into a cage. But the bird looked up at the man sadly, and began to sing:

Lyrics under the music (top line / bottom line):

Main nai kha-ya hai sain-t ka kun-ya,___ Main ka
Mine nay ky-ya hay sain-tay ka koon-ya,___ Mine ka

bhan-ta dha-ray le-hay ja-ta,___ Mo-ra nad-di ka-na-ray ba-
ba-ta da-ray lee-hay ja-ta,___ Mo-ra na-dee ka-na-ray ba-

-sa-ra,___ Mo-rey ro-te___ hon-gey___
-say-ra,___ Mo-ray ro-tay___ hong-gay-ay___

la-l ga-dai-la___ Run-g chon chon___ chon chon.
la-lay ga-day-la,___ Roon-gay choong choong___ choong choong.

Main nai khaya hai saint ka kunya
Main ka bhanta dharay lehay jata,
Mora naddi kanaray basara,
Morey rote hongey lal gadaila.
Rung chon-chon chon-chon.

(I have feasted in the millet field free.
But the birdcatcher with his net caught me,
In a nest by the river are my young,
They are crying for their mother to come.
Rung choo choo choo choo.)

Do you think the birdcatcher felt sorry for the bird? He did not! When he heard her song, sung so nicely, he just thought to himself, 'Good! The bird can sing sweetly as well as being pretty. Perhaps the Raja will give me even more money for her!'

And off he went, swinging the cage.

He hadn't gone far, when he met a shepherd. The bird looked at the shepherd sadly and began to sing:

Bheri ke charwayya bhayya,
Main nai khaya hai saint ka kunya . . .

When the shepherd heard the song, he felt sorry for the bird.

'Please, birdcatcher,' he said, 'let the poor bird go home to her nest, and I will give you one of my fine lambs.'

But the birdcatcher would not. 'I'm taking her to the Raja,' he said. 'I'll get lots of money for this bird.'

On he went, but a little further along he met a camel herder, and again the bird began to sing:

Ootan ke charwayya bhayya,
Main nai khaya hai saint ka kunya . . .

When the camel herder heard the song, his heart melted. 'Take a camel from me,' he said, 'and let that bird go free.'

But the birdcatcher would not. 'I'm going to get lots and lots of money for this bird,' he said. And on he went.

When they were near to the Raja's palace, they met a mahout with his elephants. Once more the bird sang:

Hathi ke charwayya bhayya,
Main nai khaya hai saint ka kunya . . .

Bhe- ri   ke cha-r - way-ya bhay -
Bay - ree   kay cha-re - wy - ya by -

etc.

- ya,   Main nai kha-ya hai sain-t ka
- ya,   Mine nay ky - ya hay sain-tay ka

Oo - tan   ke cha-r - way-ya bhay -
Oo - tan   kay cha-re - wy - ya by -

etc.

- ya,   Main nai
- ya,   Mine nay

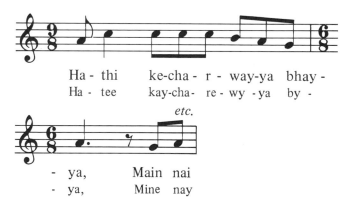

Ha - thi   ke-cha - r - way -ya bhay -
Ha - tee   kay-cha - re - wy - ya   by -

etc.

- ya,   Main nai
- ya,   Mine nay

(Oh brother shepherd,
I have feasted in the millet field . . .)

(Oh brother camel herder,
I have feasted in the millet field . . .)

(Oh brother mahout,
I have feasted in the millet field . . .)

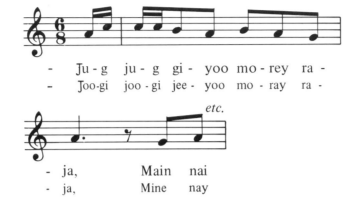

When the mahout heard the song, he felt his heart would break. 'Let that bird go,' he begged, 'and I will give you one of my elephants.'

But the birdcatcher would not. 'I'm going to get lots and lots and lots of money for this bird,' he said, and he hurried on to the palace.

When the Raja saw the bird, he was indeed pleased, and he did indeed give the birdcatcher a lot of money, and sent him away happy. When the bird saw how generous the Raja was, she began to feel hopeful.

'I have touched the heart of a shepherd, melted the heart of a camel herder, and broken the heart of a mahout,' she thought. 'Surely the Raja will be as kindhearted as they were.'

And so she sang her song once again:

**Jug jug giyoo morey raja,
Main nai khaya saint ka kunya . . .**

- Ju - g ju - g gi - yoo mo - rey ra -
- Joo-gi joo - gi jee - yoo mo - ray ra -

- ja, Main nai
- ja, Mine nay

(Oh, my king, may you live long,
I have feasted in the millet field . . .)

Do you think the Raja took pity on the bird? He did not! When he heard her song, he liked it so much he said, 'I'll never never let you go! I'll give you a golden cage and you can sing all day and all night.'

When the bird heard that, she was so disappointed she lost her temper.

'Oh my king, may you not live long at all!' she cried. 'The poorest herdsboy in your kingdom is far nobler than you!'

Now no one had ever dared to speak to the Raja like that before. He was furious! 'Hold your tongue!' he roared, 'Or I'll eat you!'

'Pluck me, eat me, do what you like,' said the bird. 'But I never will be quiet.'

So the Raja sent for the cook, and the cook took the bird to the kitchen. And he plucked her and fried her and put her on a plate. But all the time the bird kept singing.

They took her into the Raja, and he swallowed her down in one, and she still kept singing. The Raja began to feel very uncomfortable with the bird singing and dancing around in his stomach. All of a sudden he cried, 'Oh! She's coming back up! Don't let her get away!'

So all the soldiers took their swords out, and stood round waiting. And OUT came the bird, and SWIPE went the soldiers' swords. But the bird was too quick. The swords missed her altogether. They went swinging on and SWOOSH! cut off the Raja's head.

Then the bird flew up and perched on the palace wall and sang triumphantly: 'Raja's cut his head off! Raja's cut his head off! But I'm alright.'

Ah, if only the Raja had listened, he might have lived to grow wiser!

Bouki Dances the Kokioko

There was once a king of Haiti who loved dancing. He loved dancing more than anything else in the world. If he could he would have invited dancers to perform for him every evening of the week; but unfortunately, he did not have enough money in his treasury to pay them.

One evening after dinner, when the king was sitting alone in his garden, he made up a song:

**Kokioko, oh, samba,
Now I dance, now I dance like this.
Kokioko, oh, samba,
Now I dance, now I dance like this.
Samba, oh, samba, ah.**

**Samba dance, samba dance,
Samba dance, samba dance.
Samba dance, samba dance,
Samba dance, samba dance.**

He sang it several times, then he stood up. He sniffed the soft night air and, swaying from side to side, he made up a dance to match his song:

Kokioko, oh, samba ...

And the more he whirled around the more impressed he was with his own dance.

'No one could make up such a dance,' he thought to himself. 'But, of course, there are always those who think they can do anything. Maybe . . .'

The next morning, the king announced that he would pay 5,000 gourdes to anyone who could dance the kokioko. That evening, a long line of dancers, many with newly made amulets around their necks, waited outside the palace hoping they might be able to guess the steps of the kokioko. And that night, the king saw some of the most splendid dancing he had ever seen all for free, for no one, amulet or no amulet, was able to guess the steps of the kokioko.

The next night it was the same thing, and the night after. Sometimes one dancer would happen to do the first steps of the kokioko, and the king would sit up in excitement. Once, a dancer did the first and second parts of the kokioko, but then he did the wrong steps for the samba dance.

Months passed and the king never tired of watching the dancing. But always after the dancers and servants left for the evening, the king would dance the kokioko by himself, so he wouldn't forget it.

It happened that one evening, Malice, the king's gardener, returned to the palace for his hat. As he came near the garden he heard the king singing:

Kokioko, oh, samba,
Now I dance, now I dance like this.
Kokioko, oh, samba,
Now I dance, now I dance like this.
Samba, oh, samba, ah.
   Samba dance, samba dance,
   Samba dance, samba dance . . .

Malice crept up to the gate and saw the king was dancing the kokioko in the moonlight. He followed every movement with greedy eager eyes and then ran home to tell his wife, Madame Malice.

Before work the next morning, Malice went to see his friend, Bouki.

'Bouki,' he said, 'we have been friends for many years and now I am going to do something *really* great for you.'

'Oh-oh,' said Bouki. He had been friends long enough with Malice to know that when Malice started out to help you . . .

you were much better off *before* he came along. No one was trickier than Malice.

'Leave well enough alone!' said Bouki.

'Bouki, do you know what I saw last night? I saw the king dancing the kokioko in his garden. I saw every step he made. I can't dance it for him because I am his servant and he would suspect me. But I will teach you the steps and you will win the 5,000 gourdes.'

Now 5,000 gourdes is a lot of money – especially for Bouki, who had many little Boukis to feed. And also for Malice – who had many little Malices.

'Show me the dance,' said Bouki.

Malice sang and danced:

Kokioko, oh, samba . . .

Then Bouki tried to follow Malice's movements:

Koki-o-o-OH!

Bouki was so fat and awkward, he nearly fell over.

'Never mind,' said Malice. 'I'll be back tonight to teach you. We'll do a little bit every night and you'll learn.'

Two months later, Bouki and Malice joined the line of dancers waiting outside the king's palace. When it was Bouki's turn, he went in alone and danced for the king. It was a very fat dancer who danced the kokioko, but it *was* the kokioko!

Kokioko, oh, samba ...

There was no doubt about it. The king was flabbergasted, amazed, stunned, and forced to give Bouki his reward. Bouki rushed joyously out of the palace with his sack of 5,000 gourdes.

'I've won, Malice, I've won!' Bouki shouted.

Bouki and Malice walked gaily home through the forest, but as they passed a large breadfruit tree, Malice suddenly stopped and said:

'Bouki, now that you can dance the kokioko, I'm going to teach you one of the easiest dances there is.'

Malice moved his rump back and forth, closed his eyes and sang:

If you have no sense,
Put your sack on the ground
And dance. (*Repeat ad lib*)

'That's easy,' said Bouki. And he put his sack on the ground and imitated Malice:

If you have no sense,
Put your sack on the ground
And dance ...

'Good,' said Malice. And he began to sing faster and faster and shake his whole body:

If you have no sense,
Put your sack on the ground
And dance ...

Bouki did the same. And his eyes were shut tight when Madame Malice crept out from behind the breadfruit tree and picked up his sack.

If you have no sense,
Put your sack on the ground
And dance ...

Suddenly Bouki opened his eyes and looked on the ground. 'My *sack*, Malice, my SACK!'

'Oh-oh, did you put it on the gr-round?' asked Malice in mock seriousness.

'Yes, of course.'

'Oh, Bouki, no! I *tried* to warn you,' said Malice. And he disappeared into the night, singing:

If you have no sense,
Put your sack on the ground
And dance ...

If you have no sense,— Put your sack on the ground and dance.— If you have no sense, Put your sack on the ground and dance.—

The Blind Beggar

There was once a blind beggar who had a beautiful voice. Every day he went to the market place and sang – old songs, new songs, happy songs and sad songs. Many people stopped to listen, and most of them gave him money. Some gave a few lira, some gave more. Sometimes he even got a gold coin. The blind singer saved as much as he could, and little by little he grew richer, until at last he had a bag full of money jingling in his pocket. And when he counted it he found he had one hundred ducats!

Now he began to worry about all this money. Where could he put it where it would be safe? Finally he decided to go out into the countryside and find a lonely place and hide it. So off he went, very early one morning, over the hills and along the footpaths, tap-tap-tapping with his cane to tell him the way. He didn't see the farmer up early too, out working in his fields. But the farmer saw him. And the farmer watched curiously as the beggar felt under hedges and sounded out trees, looking for a hiding place. So the farmer saw him find at last the perfect spot – a hollow tree beside a stream – and watched him carefully place

his bag of gold inside. And of course, as soon as the beggar had gone, the farmer hurried up to the tree, took out the gold, and went home laughing.

When the blind beggar returned to check his treasure, he was heartbroken. He guessed that someone had seen him hide the gold, but how could he, a blind man, ever find out who it was? And even if he did, how could he get the money back? He thought and thought and thought as he felt his way, slowly and sadly, back to town. By the time he got to the market-place, he had an idea.

He waited until the market began and the place was full of people. Then he began to sing. Not his usual songs but one special song, newly made for the occasion. Over and over again he sang:

Hear me sing now of my secret fortune,
Half I hid in a bag in a hollow,
Half again I will hide there tomorrow,
Where one is sure, two are doubly secure.

Ascoltate vi dico un segreto,
Un sacco d'oro ho messo in un buco,
Un altro ancora ci metto domani,
Se uno è sicuro un' altro sará.

It was a beautiful song, and he sang it so well everyone crowded to hear. Some shook their heads at the words; some laughed. But one man did neither. It was the farmer who had taken the gold. Just as the beggar had hoped, this farmer had come to spend some of his new-found wealth. When he heard the song and recognised the beggar, he listened hard to the words:

Hear me sing now of my secret fortune...

Ascoltate vi dico un segreto...

Half —	a -	gain	I	will	hide	there	to -	mor -	row, —
Un	al -	tro an -	co -	ra	ci	met -	to	do -	ma -	ni, Se
Oon	al -	tro an -	ko -	ra	chee	me -	to	do -	ma -	nee, Si

Where one is	sure, two	are	doub- ly	se -	cure. —
u - no e si -	cu - ro	un'	al - tro	sa -	rá. —
oo - no e see -	koo - ro	oon	al - tro	sa -	ra. —

'Aha,' he thought, 'I must be clever here! When the beggar takes his second bag of gold to the hollow tree, he will check that the first bag is still there. If it is gone, he will take the second bag somewhere safer. But if I return the first bag, he will think his hiding place is still safe – and he will leave the rest of the gold there too. Ha ha ha! Tomorrow I will be doubly rich!'

So the farmer went straight back to the hollow tree, and put back the bag of gold. And when the beggar returned there, late that night, he found his money waiting for

him. Joyfully, he took it out and put it in his pocket – and there he kept it ever after, safe and sound.

As for the farmer, when he returned the next day, the tree was empty. Do you think he was pleased? He was not! He was doubly disappointed – and serve him right!

Lunga la fola stretta la via,
Dite la vostra che ho detto la mia.

Long was the path but short the way,
You tell your story now I've had my say.

Mr Hawk and Mother Hen

Once upon a time, Mr Hawk and Mother Hen shared a house. Sharing a house also means sharing the housework. But Mother Hen didn't want to do any work, even though she had nine chickens that needed to be cared for.

Poor Mr Hawk! He had to do the shopping, the cooking and the washing up by himself. In fact, he did all the housework. Mother Hen had no shame! One day she would complain of a headache, the next day a tummyache or a backache. In fact, she had nothing wrong with her at all. She just loved to sit on her newly-laid eggs and do nothing.

One particular day Mr Hawk woke up very early and looked around the house. There were dirty dishes and rubbish everywhere. 'I've had enough!' said Mr Hawk.

Before Mother Hen and her chickens could wake up and demand breakfast, Mr Hawk disappeared into the forest. He got himself a log, carried the wood home on his head, and laid it down on a stone.

Mother Hen and her chickens had woken up by this time. They looked everywhere for Mr Hawk, but couldn't find

him. Mr Hawk was hiding at the back of the house carving his log of wood.

First of all he chipped the bark off very carefully. Then he hollowed it out. When he had finished it looked like a huge tube. Next he went back into the forest. He flew between the trees until he saw what he wanted below – a dead deer. Mr Hawk swooped down, took off the skin and carried it home.

He stretched the deerskin tightly over the end of the hollowed log and hammered pegs in to hold it down.

He had made a drum! He was so pleased with himself, he whistled with pride. He

fetched an old branch and carved it into a pair of drumsticks, then left the drum in the sun to dry.

Early the next morning he picked up his drumsticks and began to play a rhythm:

Me, Kofi Babone, me ne nkoko besa,
Sensensa,
Me, Kofi Babone, me ne nkoko besa,
Sensensa,
Nkoko besa, sensensa,
Nkoko besa, sensensa,
Sensensa, sensensa, sensensa.
(Repeat last line ad lib)

Me, Ko-fi Ba-bo-ne, me ne n-ko-ko be-sa, Sen-sen-sa, N-
Mi, koe-fee ba-baw-ni, mi nin-koe-kaw bes-sa, Sen-sen-san-

Repeat ad lib

- ko-ko be-sa, Sen-sen-sa,(N-) Sen-sen-sa, sen-sen-sa, sen-sen-sa.
- koe-kaw bes-sa, Sen-sen-sa,(n-) Sen-sen-sa, sen-sen-sa, sen-sen-sa.

The chickens, hearing this wonderful drumming, flapped their wings and tried to dance. Mother Hen got up from her twelve eggs and joined them. This went on all day, then the next day too, and the day after. Mother Hen got thinner and thinner because Mr Hawk wasn't cooking anymore, but *still* she wouldn't help with the housework.

And so it went on until one fine morning when Mr Hawk decided to visit his friends and relatives. He hadn't been gone long before Mother Hen had picked up the drumsticks and begun to play the drum herself. Her chickens danced around, flapping their wings – they were experts by now:

Me, Kofi Babone, me ne nkoko besa . . .

They were enjoying themselves so much they didn't want to stop. Soon Mr Hawk was on his way back. As he got nearer he heard the drumming, and he knew that someone was playing his drum. When he came to the door of the house, he saw Mother Hen holding *his* sticks and playing *his* drum. Mr Hawk was furious. He gave Mother Hen a filthy look without saying a word. Mother Hen was afraid.

Suddenly Mr Hawk flew up to the roof of the house. Then, without warning, he dived down and grabbed one of Mother Hen's chickens. Mother Hen began to sob and plead for mercy. 'Please, please, Mr Hawk, spare my chicken. I promise to help with the housework now.'

'Too late!' said Mr Hawk.

'Very well,' said Mother Hen, 'I promise you a brand new, bright yellow chicken when I hatch my eggs.'

'I'll wait,' said Mr Hawk.

A few days later, Mr Hawk woke up early to the sound of c-r-a-c-k, c-r-a-c-k, c-r-a-c-k. All twelve of Mother Hen's eggs had cracked open, setting free twelve new lives. Mr Hawk flew up onto the roof and waited for the chickens to come out into the yard.

At noon Mother Hen brought out the new chickens to show to the older ones and Mr Hawk swooped down from the roof. The older chickens ran for their lives, and Mother Hen scooped up one new chicken in her beak. But all the rest were gobbled up by Mr Hawk.

Mother Hen and her chickens ran until they came to a nearby farm. The farmer quickly put a fence and wire netting round and over the chickens and their mother to keep Mr Hawk out.

Mr Hawk still bears Mother Hen and her chickens a grudge to this day. That is the reason why poultry farmers in Ghana have to protect their chickens by building a wire fence around their farms.

This story that you've just heard, whether it's true or not, whether you enjoyed it or not, take it away and bring back another one with you.

The Boy who Lived with the Bears

There was once a boy whose father and mother had died. The only person left to take care of him was his uncle, but his uncle's mind was not straight about his nephew. The boy had been taught by his parents always to do as his elders told him, but the uncle thought the boy was too much trouble. He fed him scraps and dressed him in tattered clothing. At night the boy had to sleep outside the lodge away from the fire. The uncle never even spoke the boy's name. He just called him 'You!' Yet that boy never complained.

One day, when the uncle woke up, there was an evil thought in his mind. 'Today,' he thought, 'I will get rid of that troublesome boy.'

He went outside to where the boy slept by the side of the lodge.

'You,' he said, 'come with me. We are going hunting.'

The boy was very happy. His uncle was a great hunter and had never taken him along before. But the boy noticed something strange.

'Aren't you going to take along your dog, Uncle?'

'No,' the uncle said. 'Today you will be the dog.'

Then they set out. Always before when he went to hunt, the uncle went to the east or the west or the south! This time, though, he went towards the north. This surprised the boy, for people said that strange things happened in the forest to the north. But he followed his uncle.

They went deeper and deeper into the woods. They went a very long way. At last they came to a clearing and on the other side of that clearing was a hill with a small cave at its base.

'You,' the uncle said to his nephew, 'crawl in and chase out any animals that are inside.'

That cave was dark, but the boy remembered what his parents had told him. He got down on his hands and knees and squeezed through the mouth of the cave. He crawled in, deeper and deeper, feeling the walls of the cave with his hands as he went. At last, he came to the end of the cave. There was nothing there, only leaves and stones. He turned to crawl back and tell his uncle that the cave was empty. But as he did so, he saw the light from the mouth of the cave disappear and all was dark. He crawled quickly back to the cave mouth. A great stone had been rolled there and it was wedged tight. The boy could not move it. Then he realised what his uncle meant to do. He would be trapped in the cave forever. He sat down and began to cry.

But as he cried, the boy began to remember something. His parents always told him that if you do good, good things will come to you. And if you need help, help will come. He stopped crying. He remembered a song which his mother taught him to sing, a song for times when you feel alone and lonely and need a friend. He began to sing that song, softly at first and then louder.

Wey-a-nah, wey-a-nah, wey-a-nah, hey
Wey-a-nah, wey-a-nah, wey-a-nah, hey
Wey-a-nah, wey-a-nah, wey-a-nah, hey
Wey hey hey yo-o-o
Wey hey hey yo.
(*Sing three times*)

But as he sang, he thought he heard someone singing back to him from the other side of the stone. He stopped and

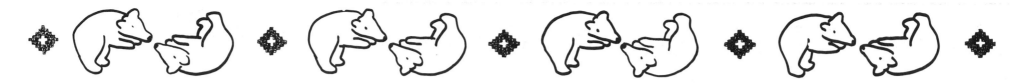

listened. Then he sang again. And now he was sure he could hear someone answering him. But it was not just one person, it was many voices. And those voices were strange. Some were very high, some were very low, some sounded like growling more than singing. They didn't sound like human voices at all:

Wey-a-nah, wey-a-nah, wey-a-nah, hey . . .

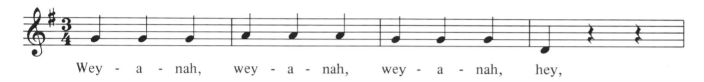

Wey - a - nah, wey - a - nah, wey - a - nah, hey,

Wey - a - nah, wey - a - nah, wey - a - nah, hey,

Wey - a - nah, wey - a - nah, wey - a - nah, hey,

Sing three times

Weh hey hey yo - o - o Wey hey hey yo.

Then, just as the song ended, the stone was rolled away from the mouth of the cave!

Blinking his eyes against the light, the boy crawled out of the cave. The clearing was full of people. There were big people and small people, people of all shapes and sizes. He blinked again and saw they were not people at all. They were animals! There was a little mole, there was a beaver, there were wolves and deer. All of the animals of the forest were there. There was even a mother bear with her cubs. An old woodchuck came up to him and nudged him in the leg.

'Grandson,' the old grandmother woodchuck said, 'we heard your song. Do you need help?'

'Yes,' said the boy. 'My parents have died and I was trapped in that cave by my uncle who doesn't want me. I have no family.'

'Then we will give you a new family,' said the old woodchuck. 'Look around this clearing. Any of the animal people here will adopt you and you can join their family.'

The boy looked around. 'I don't know how to choose,' he said. 'Could each of you

tell me what your lives are like so I can decide.'

The animals agreed and they began. The first to speak was the tiny mole.

'You would like to be a mole,' she squeaked. 'We live in a lovely hole in the ground and we burrow in the soft earth. We eat the most delicious worms you've ever tasted.'

The boy didn't like the idea of eating worms, but he remembered that he had always been taught to be polite, especially to people who offer help.

'Thank you, Mole,' the boy said, 'but I'm too big to go into your burrow and my hands aren't made for digging like your strong paws. I could never be a mole.'

The beaver came up to him next.

'Grandson,' the beaver chirped, 'you would certainly like our life. We swim underwater and live in a nice lodge. There we eat the tastiest tree bark you could ever imagine.'

The boy didn't like the thought of eating tree bark, but he remembered his manners.

'Thank you, Beaver,' the boy said, 'but I can't hold my breath very long underwater and I don't have a strong tail as you do to help me swim. I could never be a beaver.'

So each of the animals came and described their lives. The deer talked about leaping through the forest over the fallen trees, the wolf spoke of hunting after the other animals. Each of the animals told about their life and none of them seemed quite right. Then the old mother bear walked up to the boy. She looked at him a long time before speaking and when she did speak her voice was like a growling song.

'You would like to be a bear,' she said. 'We take our time going through the forest and none of the other animals get in our way. Our voices are rough, but our hearts are warm. We eat honey and the sweetest berries and our den is warm. If you decide to be a bear, my cubs will wrestle and play with you as much as you wish.'

'I will be a bear!' the boy said.

So the boy went to live with the bears. It was just as the mother bear said. They took their time going through the forest. They ate berries and honey and slept in a warm den and the cubs played with him to his heart's content. But one strange thing happened. Whenever the cubs scratched him as they played, long black hair grew on the boy's body. Before long, he was covered with hair and looked like a bear himself.

Their life went on this way for a long time. Then, one day, as they were gathering berries, the old mother bear told them to be silent.

'Listen,' she said, 'listen. There is a hunter in the forest!'

They all listened and soon the boy heard something. He heard the sounds of a man walking heavily through the woods, breaking twigs and shuffling through the leaves.

'Hunh-hunh-hunh!' the mother bear laughed, 'that is a hunter we do not have to fear. That is the hunter who makes so much noise going through the forest that the twigs and leaves speak of him wherever he goes. He never sees any animals and we call him Heavy-Foot.'

Another day, as they fished in the stream, the old mother bear told them again to be quiet.

'Listen,' she said, 'listen. Another hunter is in the forest.'

They all listened and soon the boy heard something. He heard the sound of a man talking and singing. The man talked and sang of what a great hunter he was!

'Hunh-hunh-hunh!' the mother bear laughed. 'That one is not dangerous. He makes so much noise with his bragging and his songs that all the animals hide from him. Such men forget that everything in the forest has ears. We bears can hear singing, even if it is only thought and not spoken. We call that hunter Flapping-Jaws.'

So it went. Each time a hunter came into the woods the old mother bear listened and laughed. One day they heard the hunter called Loses-His-Weapons, another day they heard Bumps-Into-Trees. None of those hunters were dangerous. None of them could catch a bear.

One day, though, the old mother bear stopped them. 'Listen,' she said, 'listen.'

They listened but could hear nothing at first. Then, very faintly, the boy heard footsteps. But it sounded like more than just two feet and the steps were very soft.

The old mother bear looked worried. 'It is the one we fear,' she said. 'It is Two-Legs-And-Four-Legs. When Two-Legs-And-Four-Legs hunt any animal, they never stop until they catch it. We must run!'

Then she began to run, making the boy and her cubs run ahead of her. They ran through the forest. From behind them came the sound of the hunting cry of Four-Legs. They ran through the swamps. But the sound of Two-Legs-And-Four-Legs was closer now behind them. They ran up the hills and through the ravines, they ran through the thorn bushes and across the streams, but they could not escape. The awful sound of the hunting cry of Four-Legs was close at their heels. At last they came into a clearing. There was a big hollow log.

'Crawl inside,' said the mother bear. 'We must hide.'

They crawled into the hollow log and waited. Soon the boy heard Four-Legs sniffing and scratching at the log. Then he heard Two-Legs walking around the log.

Then everything was quiet. He thought perhaps they had gone away, but then he smelled something. It was smoke! Two-Legs had made a fire at the end of the log and was blowing the smoke inside to force them to come out.

That was when the boy remembered something. He remembered that he was really a human being and that Two-Legs was a human hunter.

'Stop!' the boy shouted. 'Don't hurt my family.'

The smoke stopped coming into the log. The boy crawled out, blinking his eyes against the light. There in front of him stood Two-Legs and Four-Legs, the hunter and his dog. And the hunter was his uncle!

The uncle stepped forward and touched the boy. As soon as he touched him, all of the long black hair fell off and he looked like a boy again.

'My nephew,' said the uncle, 'is it truly you or are you a ghost?'

'I am alive, Uncle,' the boy said.

'My nephew,' the uncle said, 'I was a wicked man. When I left you in that cave, my mind was crooked. As soon as I got back to our lodge I realised what a wicked

thing I had done. I ran back to set you free, but you were gone. There were the tracks of many animals and I thought they had eaten you.'

'The animals helped me, Uncle. The bears have taken care of me. They are my family. Do not hurt them.'

The uncle tied his dog to a tree. 'Bring out your friends,' he said. 'I will be the friend of all bears from this moment on.'

So the boy called out the mother bear and her cubs. They came out slowly and spoke to the boy with words which sounded at first to the uncle like nothing more than the growling of an animal. Yet, as he listened more closely, he, too, could understand.

'Grandson,' the old mother bear said, 'we will always be your relatives. You must always remember the warmth in an animal's heart.'

So it was that the boy and his uncle came to live together happily. And they were friends to the bears for as long as they lived.

The Singing Sack

Once, in a hot sleepy town in Andalucia, there lived a widow and her little daughter. They weren't rich, but they were happy together. And the girl had one treasure – a beautiful bright pink coral necklace. She wore it all the time, wherever she went, and she was always very careful not to lose or break it.

Now, in the middle of the town there was a fountain where everyone went to fetch their water. It flowed out clean and fresh and ran into a deep trough where people could dip their water-pots or pitchers. Every night and every morning, the little girl went for the water, but because she was so small she had to lean right in to fill her pot. As she was afraid that her necklace would slip off, and fall into the water, she always laid it safely on a special stone until she was ready to go home.

One evening, as she was heaving the heavy pot up out of the water, she suddenly felt that someone was watching her. She looked round, and there behind her, she saw the most horrible creature grinning and winking and sidling towards her. It was a huge and horrible ogre,

wrinkled as a walnut, yellow as a lemon and dressed in rags. The little girl was so scared, she took the pot and ran – and she didn't remember until she was half way home, that she'd left her coral necklace behind, lying by the fountain.

She didn't want to go back – but she didn't want to lose that necklace – it was so beautiful, and she loved it so much. She turned this way and that, thinking yes, thinking no, but at last she made up her mind. She put down the pot, took a deep breath and marched bravely back to the fountain.

The ogre was still there, waiting, and in his hand, held out towards her, was her bright pink coral necklace.

'You forgot this,' he said. 'Come here and get it.'

The girl didn't want to, but she did want that necklace. She reached out to grab it – but the ogre was faster. Quick as a flash he caught the girl with one hand, and with the other he pulled out a sack from behind his back.

'Now you'll come in useful,' he said, popping her inside. 'You can sing for my supper!'

Off he went to the nearest house and banged on the door.

'I've got a wonderful thing!' he cried. 'A magical singing sack! Listen here, and pay me well!'

When the people came out he shook the sack and whispered fiercely, 'Sing, singing sack – or I'll give you a smack!'

And the little girl inside the sack had to sing:

I'm my mother's only daughter,
Now she is alone, all alone, all alone.
She sent me to fetch her the water,
Now I can't get home, can't get home,
 can't get home.

Soy la unica hija de mi mamá,
Sola muy sola ella estará.
Fui a la fuente el agua traer,
Ahora a mi casa no puedo regresar.

The girl sang so sweetly and sadly, everyone loved to hear it.

'What a wonderful magical singing sack,' they cried, and they gave the ogre lots of food and money.

I'm my mo-ther's on-ly daugh-ter,
Soy la u-ni-ca hi-ja de mi ma-má,
Soy la oo-nee-ka ee-ha de mee ma-ma,

Now she is a-lone all a-lone all a-lone.
So la muy so-la el-la es-ta-rá.
Soe la mooe soe-la el-ya es-ta-ra.

She sent me to fetch her the wa—ter,
Fui a la fuen-te el a-gua tra—er,
Fwee-a la fwen-tay el a-gwa tra—air,

Now I can't get home, can't get home, can't get home.
Aho-ra a mi ca-sa no pue-do re-gre-sar.
Ao-ra mee ca-za noe pooay-do re-gre-sar.

So the wicked creature went from house to house, and the girl had to sing again and again, until her voice was cracked and hoarse, and she was so tired and cramped inside the sack, she ached all over.

But little by little, house by house, the ogre worked his way up the hill, until at last they came to the house of the little girl herself.

When the girl's mother came to the door, and the ogre shook the sack, the girl sang even more sweetly, and even more sadly:

I'm my mother's only daughter ...

Soy la unica hija de mi mamá ...

Instantly, the widow recognised her missing daughter's voice. But what could she do? – the ogre was huge and strong. She thought quickly, then said, 'What a lovely song! How clever you must be, sir, to teach a sack to sing like that! Surely you must have magic powers! You must be very special!'

She kept on thanking and flattering the ogre, and the more she said, the more he wanted to hear – she made him feel so pleased with himself. And meanwhile she gave him drink after drink, bottle after bottle of thick strong wine and brandy. And he drank, and drank, and drank until at last he fell down in a heap and began to snore.

Quickly, the mother undid the sack and out jumped the little girl. They hugged each other and wept for joy, then the woman took her daughter and hid her away safe and sound inside the house. Into the sack she put a big dog and a cross cat, and then she tied the top up carefully just as it had been before.

By and by the ogre woke up – and how his head ached! He was in a terrible temper. He grabbed the sack and strode off to the next town, and once again went round calling people to listen to his magical singing sack.

But this time, when he whispered, 'Sing, singing sack – or I'll give you a smack!' nothing happened; no one sang at all. The people smiled and shook their heads and the ogre got very cross. He shook the sack furiously and cried, 'Sing, singing sack – or you'll get such a whack!'

The cat and the dog didn't like being shaken, and so they began to complain. The dog barked – Bow Wow! The cat mewed – Miouw! And everyone laughed and laughed.

Now the ogre was really furious! He thought the girl was still in the sack, trying to make a fool of him.

'I'll teach you!' he yelled as he hurried out of town to find a quiet spot where he could open the sack.

But when he did, what a shock he got! Out leapt the dog snarling and biting, out scrambled the cat scratching and spitting. Off ran the ogre as fast as he could, with the furious animals hard on his heels.

Maybe they caught him, maybe they didn't, but one thing is for certain – he never came back. And that was the end of that.

Sambalele

There was an old woman who lived in a hut in a clearing in the great Amazon forest. She was an old woman, but she was also very strong and very capable. She built the house herself and planted a garden around it. A garden with all kinds of fruit and vegetables. Some you know, like pumpkins, beans and peas, and some you may never have seen, like cassavas, mangoes and papayas. Every morning, after looking after the garden, she used to go to the river to fish.

Now, somewhere far away in the forest, there lived Sambalele. Sambalele was a little monkey, and he lived with his tribe in a very dense and overgrown patch of forest. Sambalele wasn't a very nice monkey. He was very mischievous, always playing little jokes (which were not very amusing) on the other monkeys, like for example setting their tails on fire. One day, Sambalele, bored and having done every kind of mischief he could think of, decided that he was going to leave his tribe and go in search of adventure. So, to the general relief and happiness of the whole tribe, off he went.

Well, he jumped from tree to tree for a whole day, then he slept in a very big tree. Next morning, refreshed, he continued travelling, far and far away. And at the end of the third day he found the clearing. He looked at the house with great interest and then he realised that there was a garden full of the most amazing and beautiful fruit and vegetables that he had ever seen in his life. His eyes opened as wide as saucers in his head.

At that time of the day, as usual, the woman was down at the river fishing, washing clothes and swimming. And since Sambalele found that there was no one around, he dived headfirst into the middle of the garden, and began eating everything he could lay his four hands on, (because you know monkeys have four hands, they don't have feet like ours). He plucked everything he could, even fruit that was still green, and he ate so much that after a while he crawled very slowly on his belly back into the bush, where he lay sick for a few hours.

The sun went down and the old woman came back from the river with two very big fish that she had caught, and a pile of neat and clean clothes in a basket on her head.

She came into the clearing and immediately noticed the destruction. Everything was torn apart, fruit thrown all over the place, vegetables strewn, young seedlings scattered and trampled on. She was so surprised and shocked that she let the basket fall from her head, and the fish fell to the ground. She was in such distress, she almost cried. But she was a very strong woman, so instead of crying she looked very carefully all around, and thought, 'This mischief could only have been done by a monkey. I have no monkeys around here, but there must be a monkey somewhere that has come into my garden and created this destruction.'

So there and then she decided that she was going to get that monkey. She picked up some logs and went into her hut closing the door after her. All night you could hear her working away and the lights and the fire kept on burning and burning while she hammered and worked and put things together. When the sun came up the old woman, very tired but happy, came out into the garden with a doll which looked just like a little five-year old girl. This was what she'd spent the night making. She

took a pot of tar, and painted the doll all over so she was sticky from head to toe. Then she took this lovely little girl with a nice grin on her face and stood her in the middle of the garden. Very pleased with herself, the woman took up her clothes and her fishing rod and went back to the river.

At twelve o'clock, Sambalele woke up and started scratching his face. He'd had a very uncomfortable night, because he'd eaten so much. Nevertheless, all he could think of was going back to the garden and eating some more. So he crawled back to the garden, jumped into the middle, and was stuffing his mouth with corn and mangoes when he suddenly realised that someone was looking at him. O-oh. Maybe he had been caught. So he turned and looked and there was this very nice looking little girl, grinning from ear to ear. Sambalele thought, 'Well, I can eat some more later, maybe I should go and ask if this girl will play with me.'

After all, he was very lonely being away from all the monkeys he knew, having no one to talk to and no one to brag to. So he went to the little girl and said, 'Good morning, little girl, I am Sambalele. I am a

very important monkey in my tribe. I am very clever, very intelligent, very rich, and I jump from the tallest of the trees.'

And he went on boasting like this, and finally asked the little girl (who was, of course, silent), 'What's your name?'

The girl just grinned.

'Well,' said Sambalele, 'maybe you'd like to play with me. We could run around the garden, then we could go and try to find something interesting to eat, and perhaps we could sing some songs together.'

The little girl stayed silent.

So Sambalele said, 'Hey, haven't you got any manners? I'm talking to you. Won't you answer me?'

But the little girl just grinned.

'Listen, when I talk to you you should answer me, because I am Sambalele, a very clever and important monkey. Answer me! I'm getting very annoyed with you.'

He stamped his feet with impatience.

Now of course all the girl did was grin her lovely wide smile behind the tar. So Sambalele smacked her very hard in the face, and to his surprise his hand stuck.

'Let go of me!' he said. 'Let go of me, or I'll smack you again!'

But the girl just grinned, so he smacked her on the other side of her face, and to his surprise his other hand stuck.

'Let go,' he said, 'or I'll kick you!'

So he kicked her, and his foot stuck fast. More furious than ever, he kicked her with his other foot, and that foot stuck too.

'You stupid little girl, let me go or I'll hit you with my head!'

So he hit her with his head, and that got stuck. Finally, he switched his tail at her, and now . . . he was completely stuck!

At sundown the old woman came back and as she came into the garden she heard the howling and screaming of Sambalele. Now, this time she had a bamboo stick with her and she was smiling.

'Well,' she said to Sambalele, 'so *you* are the pest who has been destroying my garden and eating the green fruit and breaking my plants. You are the nasty thing who destroys what you cannot eat and breaks what you cannot take away. Right, now I've got something for you.'

And she gave him such a whack on his bottom that Sambalele broke free from the tar girl with a yell and a scream. But his tail was stuck so fast that it wouldn't come

away. He pulled so hard, it broke off, and he ran into the forest, leaving it behind. He didn't stop running until he got to his tribe of monkeys, to whom he told his tale – very much changed.

'Ah,' he said, 'I'm so glad to be back. I've been in a terrible place, a place in the forest where there lives a sorceress and her daughter. The daughter doesn't speak, and the sorceress is thirty feet tall!'

But all the monkeys laughed and sang, and made mockery of his story. He was a monkey without a tail! The other monkeys made up a song about him which said:

Sambalele is sick, he has a sore head.
Sambalele deserves a handful of smacks!

Sambalêlê 'tá doente,
Tá com a cabeça amarrada,
Sambalêlê bem merece,
Uma porção de palmadas.

Samba, Samba, Samba ó lêlê,
Samba, Samba, Samba ó lálá,
Samba, Samba, Samba ó lêlê,
Na barra da saia ó lálá.
(*Repeat ad lib and fade.*)

Sam-ba - lê-lê 'tá do-en - te,— Tá co'a ca-be-ça_a - mar-ra - da,—
Sam-ba - lay-lay ta doo-en - chee,— Ta kwa ka bay-sa - mar-ha - da,—

Sam-ba - lê-lê bem me-re - ce,— U - ma por-ção de pal-ma - das._
Sam-ba - lay-lay bem mer-hair - see,— Oo-ma por-saow jee pal-ma - da.—

Sam - ba, Sam - ba, Sam-ba_ó lê-lê, Sam - ba, Sam - ba, Sam-ba_ó lá-lá,
Sam - ba, Sam - ba, Sam-b'o lay-lay, Sam - ba, Sam - ba, Sam-b'o la-la,

Sam - ba, Sam - ba, Sam-ba_ó lê-lê, Na bar - ra da saia_ó lá-lá.
Sam - ba, Sam - ba, Sam-b'o lay-lay, Na ba - ha da sy - o la-la.

Annancy, Puss and Ratta

You know what 'facety' means? It's real, barefaced cheekiness. And that's how Bredda Ratta was, once upon a time, a real 'facety fella'. He was always dressed up in the latest style, and going about showing off himself. And he always thought he was better than anyone else.

So now, one day, Bra Annancy decided to teach him a lesson, to 'lowerate' him. Then Bra Annancy memba that Bredda Ratta loved to dance – he'd dance till he dropped, he couldn't stop.

So Bra Annancy got together with Bredda Puss, and they made out that they were going to have a big dance. And Bra Annancy was the fiddler. And as Bredda Ratta walk into the room, Annancy start to play a sweet tune upon the fiddle:

Ying de ying de ying,
Ying de ying de ying,
Take care you go talk oh,
Min' you tattler tongue, ying de ying,
Min' you tattler tongue, ying de ying,
Min' you tattler tongue, ying de ying.

Ying de ying de ying, Ying de ying de ying,

take care you go talk oh,

min' you tat-ler tongue, ying de ying,

min' you tat-ler tongue, ying de ying,

min' you tat-ler tongue, ying de ying.

Now Bredda Ratta was dressed up in the latest fashion, and his trousers were tight tight upon him. But when he hear the sweet sweet music, he just had to dance. And he did wheel and turn and wiggle and wind, until everybody else stop dancing to watch Bredda Ratta and praise him up. So Bredda Ratta, his head swelled to hear it, and he danced all the more. And Bra Annancy, he played faster and faster:

Ying de ying de ying ...

And then Bra Annancy change tune, and he go faster and sweeter still, and this tune says:

Bandywichy wich, bandywichy wich,
bandywichy wich,
Timber hang an' fall la la, fall la la, fall la ...

Ban-dy-wich-y wich, ban-dy-

-wich-y-wich, ban-dy wich-y wich,

Tim-ber hang an' fall la la,

Repeat ad lib. getting faster

fall la la, fall la,

And Bredda Ratta, he showed off and he wiggled and he wheeled so, till all of a sudden his trousers they go POP! and he fall on the floor.

Everyone burst out laughing, and Ratta – Lord! the shame him shame so! He ran into a hole for to hide. And from that day to today, Ratta has always lived in holes.
Is Annancy mek it so.

A Tale For Our Time

Once upon a time – and a time like now! – there was a shopkeeper who had two children, a boy and a girl.

The girl, whose name was Jacqui, was only about six years old, and the boy was much older, so he was always having to look after her, and take her to school with him in the morning, and bring her home again after, and so on. And sometimes he got a bit tired of it, always having her tagging along like that.

One winter-time, when the days were cold and dark, they were on their way home from school, when Jacqui's brother met up with school friends. He started to walk along with them, talking and laughing, and he was so busy enjoying himself he didn't notice he was going too fast for his sister to keep up.

Then he turned one corner, she turned another, and in no time at all she was lost. Jacqui hurried on, this way and that, hoping to catch up with him, but the further she went the more lost she got, until at last she came to a dead end in a strange street full of tall grey houses. Already it was getting dark, and Jacqui was getting scared. She stopped in front of

a house, wondering whether to go and ask for help, but a cat hissed crossly from on top of a fence, and sent her hurrying on. She tried to go back the way she had come, but now she couldn't remember which way it was. Then a dog began barking furiously, and she jumped, trembling, and began to run. Here and there, round and round she scurried frantically. There were one or two people about, but no one looked very helpful, or friendly enough to care about a lost little girl. They hurried past without a glance, not even seeing the large tears that rolled down Jacqui's cheeks.

Then, all at once, the street lights came on and for a moment the street didn't look quite so strange or frightening. Jacqui stopped by a lamp post to rest in the little pool of light and get her breath back. But now, when she looked on beyond it, the dark seemed twice as dark and the shadows twice as mysterious. Anything could be waiting there, ready to jump out at her. All the monsters she had ever imagined, all the ghost stories she had ever heard, came crowding into her mind, sending cold fingers down her back. And then, suddenly, out of the corner of her

eye, she saw something crouching right behind her, ready to spring. She whirled round in a panic, and the thing leapt sideways. She waved her arms and stopped. It waved and stopped as well. Then with a sigh of relief she realised what it was. Phew! It was only her shadow!

'Ha!' she sighed. 'That scared me.'

'It scared me, too,' said the shadow.

Jacqui could hardly believe her ears. She looked around, but there was no one else about. She rubbed her eyes and stared at the shadow. The shadow rubbed and stared as well.

'You spoke,' said Jacqui.

'So did you,' the shadow pointed out.

'Yes,' said Jacqui, 'but people *can* speak.'

'Oh charming,' said the shadow, bunching up into an offended sort of shape. 'So people can speak and shadows can't, eh? Says who?'

'Oh,' said Jacqui, 'I don't know.'

Then she stopped because she didn't know what to say. And she didn't want to upset this strange new friend, who at least was someone to talk to. So she just shrugged and sniffed a bit, too, because it was all so strange, and anyway, she was

still lost.

'Stop that sniffling!' snapped the shadow. 'It sounds like a cold, and that always leads to sneezing. And there's nothing worse for shadows than sneezes. Have you ever watched your shadow when you sneezed, little girl? It gets blown to pieces.'

'Oh,' said Jacqui again, but she stopped sniffing anyway. 'I'm lost, you see,' she explained. 'I lost my brother and then I lost myself.'

'So I see,' said the shadow calmly. 'But you don't seem to be doing much about getting yourself unlost, do you?'

'I don't know how to find myself,' Jacqui began, but then she gave up. She was feeling much too confused herself to be able to explain anything. The shadow shook its head.

'Tut, tut,' it said, 'don't give up! When in doubt, find out.'

Jacqui stood and thought about that for a minute, and wanted to hear if there was any more to it. But the shadow said nothing. After a while, Jacqui realised it had gone to sleep and was snoring gently.

'But, shadow!' she said at last, as loudly and as crossly as she dared. 'How? How do I find out?'

The shadow snuffled and shivered and shifted and grumbled a bit, but in the end it whispered sleepily, 'Ssh, shh, tush, tush. Silly! You just sing!'

And in a soft, husky voice it began:

(Verse 1)
When I meet a mean Kibungo,
Or tricky spider-man,
If a demon dares defy me,
Then I do what I can.

  (Chorus 1)
  I know how to trick and slip them,
  Look out! there she goes.
  Dive and dodge and dance around them,
  Keep them on their toes.

(Verse 2)
When I'm ogled by an ogre,
Or troubled by a troll,
Or groaned at by a ghostie,
Why I don't care at all!

  (Chorus 2)
  I just laugh and click my fingers,
  Ha ha! Click! click! click!
  Stamp my feet and stick my tongue out,
  That gets rid of it!

As it sang, the shadow jerked and jumped about, waving its fingers and laughing. Jacqui joined in as best she could, learning the words as she went along. She began to feel better already, and by the time they'd sung the song six times, she was stamping and laughing as happy as could be. She had almost forgotten that she was lost, and she certainly didn't worry about it.

Meanwhile, however, first her brother, and then her father, and then all the customers in his shop, and finally half the neighbours in the street had found out that little Jacqui was indeed lost. And they *did* worry. In one mad rush, they all raced back towards the school, searching every side-road, asking everyone they met, shouting and calling 'Jacqui-i-i!'. Then suddenly Jacqui's father stopped. 'Ssh!' he said, holding his hand up. 'Listen!'

And faintly, on the breeze, they heard a voice singing cheerfully:

When I meet a mean Kibungo . . .

With a whoop of delight, the search party hurried towards the song. Left, right,

left again, and now they could hear it clearly:

When I'm ogled by an ogre . . .

As they turned the last corner, they saw Jacqui. But she didn't even notice them. She was too busy singing and clicking and tapping toes with her shadow. Of course, Jacqui's family thought she was crazy, especially when she made them say hello to her shadow friend.

'Say something, shadow,' she said, 'like you said to me.'

But the shadow just lay there, as shadows do, and didn't make a sound.

'But it sang and talked and taught me the song!' cried Jacqui.

Everyone laughed, and shook their heads.

'Impossible!' they said. 'Shadows can't speak!'

'Says who?' asked Jacqui. 'And if shadows can't speak, then how did I learn that song?'

And no one knew how to answer that!

Except for Jacqui herself.

And she told me.
And I've told you.
Now you know, too.
So tell someone new!

When I   meet   a mean Ki - bun-go,   Or   tri - cky spi - der- man,   If   a
When I'm   o - gled by an o - gre,   Or   troub-led by a   troll,   Or

de - mon dares de -fy   me,   Then   I   do   what I   can.
groaned at by   a   ghos- tie,   Why   I   don't care at   all!

I   know how to   trick and slip them,   Look out! there she goes.
I   just laugh and click   my fin - gers,   Ha   ha! Click! click! click!

Dive   and dodge and dance   a - round them, Keep   them on their toes.
Stamp my feet and stick   my tongue out, That   gets rid of   it!

About the Illustrations

The techniques used to illustrate the stories were specially chosen to encourage children to explore design for themselves. Mary Currie, who runs printing workshops for young children in London, tried the techniques out with children in two schools and the illustrations on this page are examples of their work. The children were first told the stories and then invited to try out a number of techniques to illustrate them using their own impressions of the stories as starting points.

The techniques are described below for others to try. Some are more complicated than others but all can be the starting point for development by children of all ages.

Paper cutting (see *Colin's Cattle, The Blind Beggar, Mr Hawk and Mother Hen*). The sharp contrast of black and white paper is eye-catching. Any scrap paper can be used and children can experiment with different shapes and colours, and see the way a composite image can be built from separate elements.

Paper weaving (see *Gluskabi and the Wind Eagle*). A wide variety of patterns can be achieved by weaving differently coloured strips of paper.

Tissue paper montage (see *Why the Grass Never Stops Growing*). In this border tissue paper was cut into very thin strips and then arranged onto the glued paper. Tissue paper is a good material for collage work as, when it overlaps, gradations of tone occur – particularly attractive when using papers of different colours.

Tracing paper (see *Quilla Bung, The Boy who Lived with the Bears, Did the Rum Do?*). An obvious technique for repeated patterns.

Stencilling (see *Nyangara* and *The Lion on the Path*). Acetate, being transparent, is an excellent material for stencils. Repeated patterns can be lined up easily as you can see where you are in relation to the previous drawing. The sharp blades which are necessary for cutting acetate can only be used with older children under strict supervision. However simpler stencils can be made from any fairly stiff card or paper using scissors, hole punches, or simply by tearing.

Rubbings – the sacking weave on the cover was done by rubbing paper with a wax crayon over a piece of hessian. The same technique was used to illustrate *The Boy who Lived with the Bears*. Indian beadwork was the backing for this. The background to the illustration of *The Raja's Secret* is a rubbing of one of Mary's floorboards.

Fingerprinting (see *The Finger Lock*). Any paint or ink can be used and any number of digits. One child suggested creating the effect of a bagpipe with a hand print. The prints can be cut up and rearranged into any design you like.

String block printing (see *Spider the Drummer*). Take an off-cut of wood, any shape or size, and cover one surface with glue (Prittstick, PVA, etc). Press string onto the surface in the chosen pattern – the string can be moved about while the glue is still wet. When dry the string creates a raised surface which easily absorbs ink. The type of string you use will affect the result – choose from thick or thin string, smooth or coarse. Block printing ink can be sponged on, or a pad can be made by placing felt over some ink in a dish – press the block into it.

Polystyrene printing (see *The Night Troll, The Lonely Mermaid*). Ceiling tiles with their rough surface create an interesting effect when they are used for printing – apply block printing ink with a sponge or brush, then cut up the printed paper into shapes to suit your design. Smooth polystyrene, which can be bought in sheets from craft suppliers or salvaged from fruit packaging, can be incised with a pen point, or even a fingernail. Cover the area with block printing ink and press onto paper. The result is similar to that of a lino-cut, but the process is much easier and safer to use with young children.

Origins, Participation and Pronunciation

Wood block printing – when ink is applied to the ends of sawn wood, some interesting effects can be achieved, for instance the misty quality in the background to *All Skin and Bone*. In the border to *Kibungo*, the grain on a wood block was chiselled out to accentuate the pattern. This was then printed onto paper, and the paper was cut up into shapes suggesting the tall trees of a dense forest. The animals, cut from black paper, were woven in and out of them.

Printing with other objects (see *The Lonely Mermaid*). The bracken pattern in *The Lonely Mermaid* was printed directly from bracken fronds. Care needs to be taken in applying the ink – too much and it will smudge. Use a paint brush, or ink pad. All kinds of textured objects can be used – shells, feathers, fabrics, and so on.

Combining techniques (see *Sambalele*, *Kibungo* and others). More and more possibilities present themselves when you start to combine the techniques suggested above. Try out your own ideas and look for further inspiration in traditional decorative techniques.

Pronunciation. All editorial guidance on pronunciation uses sounds based on Queen's English. Where a pronunciation guide is given in small print below the melody line, the following sounds have been used:

a as in hat, *e* as in met, *i* as in pit, *o* as in hot, *u* as in but.
ai as in air, *aw* as in ought, *ee* as in feet, *oe* as in ode, *oi* as in toy, *oo* as in too, *ow* as in how, *by sy* etc as in sigh.

These sounds do not always apply to other songs and the pronunciation notes below will show where they are different. Where syllables are elided, the sign ∪ joins the words.

Gluskabi and the Wind Eagle – retold by Joseph Bruchac III (Abenaki/Slovak storyteller, writer and poet). The story is from the Abenaki tradition, while the songs are both from the Seneca tradition and are given here as sung by Joe Bruchac and the Ray Fadden family.

Accompany the songs as follows:

First song – sing three times

First time:

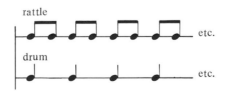

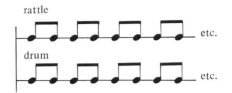

Second time:

rattle

etc.

drum

etc.

Third time: as for second time. Finish at the pause sign and let the voice fall off downward.

Second song – sing three times
First time: shake a rattle throughout
Second time: add a drum playing the strong beats

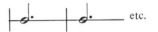 etc.

Third time: play the drum and rattle on the strong beats, and on the last 'ho' shake the rattle, play a drum roll and let the voice fall off downward.

The children can mime paddling movements like Gluskabi struggling against the wind, then breathless in the hot still air.

The words of the first song mean 'We give thanks for the corn', but vocables which are not translatable are also mixed in. The words of the second song are all vocables.

Pronunciation:	*o* as in ode
a as in hut	*ai* as in eye
ah as in car	*ey* as in hay
eh as in net	*ui* sounds ooay
i as in key	*ki* as in eye

The Finger Lock – Andra Stewart was a piper/storyteller whose version of this story was recorded

by the School of Scottish Studies, Edinburgh. Our version has been adapted slightly.

The Fairy Dance is a traditional Scottish dance tune such as the fairy might have played to cheer up Johnnie. Both this and *The Finger Lock* can be played by children on recorders with a constant drone accompaniment on the note A, which can be played on a violin, treble recorders playing in relay, or by voices humming. *The Finger Lock* is a pibroch, which is a traditional form of variations on a theme, played on the Scottish bagpipes. Only the theme of the pibroch is given here – as it goes on the tune is repeated several times with different embellishments and in variations of the basic melody. (Because of the range of the bagpipes, the version of *The Fairy Dance* played on the cassette differs slightly from the tune in its best known form, which is given here.)

Spider the Drummer – retold by Folo Graff (storyteller and musician from Sierra Leone). Folo uses this story as a basis for drama work. He invites the children to be the guests at the party; one by one they mime dipping their calabashes into the water, which is the signal for the music to begin, and then they join the ever-increasing group of hypnotised dancers.

The words of the song are in Pidgin, which is a mixture of languages. The meaning is roughly – 'Someone has done this mischief to me' i.e. Spider's expression of his grievance.

Pronunciation:
do me so sounds doo mee soe
eh as in yet

Quilla Bung – there are many versions of this story;

this particular version comes from Maryland, America. The original melody was lost, and this new setting of the words is by Sandra Kerr.

The death and resurrection of a wild goose was a common symbol of the spirit of the Black American slave.

Nyangara the Python – retold by Hugh Tracey (ethnomusicologist and storyteller) with music transcribed by Andrew Tracey. This is a story from the Shona people of Zimbabwe, and the song is in the Karanga dialect.

Treat the line 'Nyangara chena' as a chorus to be sung by the children, while the other lines of the song can be sung over it by the storyteller.

Pronunciation:
e as in ate   *u* as in too
i as in key   *ai* as in eye

The Lonely Mermaid – retold by Betsy Whyte (Scottish writer, storyteller and traveller). The song here was remembered and sung by Betsy as part of this story learnt from her mother, although the School of Scottish Studies points out that the song also belongs in a completely different context as part of another tale about the little people. It is a very haunting melody which can be punctuated by a regular hauling motion – as if pulling bracken. The children might like to try the chorus ('Pulling bracken, pulling bracken . . .') before tackling the whole song. The Gaelic pronunciation is given with the melody. Slough is pronounced *sloch* as in *loch*.

Momo-taro-san – retold by Vivienne Corringham (singer/storyteller from Lincolnshire) who heard it in rural Japan. There are many versions of this

story. 'Momo' means peach; Taro is a popular boy's name in Japan; 'san' is a term of respect like Master, Mr or Mrs.

Vivienne usually asks the children to sing only the words 'Momo-taro-san' and 'kibidango' until they are familiar with all the words and can join in with the whole song. Remember when telling the story to give the children time to answer the frequent questions in the text.

Pronunciation:
ai as in eye
i within a word sounds as in pit
i at the end sounds as in key
u as in too
h in hitotsu sounds breathy, with the lips formed as
  if to whistle

Bhambhutia – retold by Chandrika Bheda. There are many versions of this story, found all over India and Pakistan. Sometimes the old woman hides in a drum and rolls along with a drum rhythm. Different endings are even more numerous.

The rhymes are spoken in a sing song chant, and because they are so often repeated they are easy for the children to learn. *Doolook doolook* (roley poley) demands some accompanying hand rolling movements. The old woman's stick can be mimicked with a woodblock, and her voice in the bhambhutia can be suggested by chanting into loosely cupped hands.

Pronunciation:
a as in cheet*ah*
aa – both sound as in car, and both are sounded
e at the end of a word as in the French é
i as in feet
ng as in a nasal sounding *n*

th does not sound as in thank; the *h* adds a breathier sound to the *t*, as it does to *dha bhambhutia* is pronounced bham*bhoot*ia, but it is written as it normally would be in Roman script.

In this story as in *The Raja's Secret*, we have departed a little from the standard way of rendering Gujarati script into Roman script, in order to bring it more in line with the phonetic guidance given for other songs in the book.

Did the Rum Do? – retold by Kevin Graal (storyteller in the Irish tradition) from a musical anecdote by Seamus Ennis (recorded and released by Folktracks and Sound Post Publications, 1982, on a cassette called *John Airy: Stories and Pipe Tunes*).

Kevin uses this story to teach children the basics of lilting. The phrase 'did the rum do' introduces them to some of the basic syllables used in lilting, and it is easy to remember. Thereafter, other syllables can be introduced gradually as in the second half which develops the first phrase. Get the children to repeat each line of the lilt as it is said by the storyteller.

The Night Troll – retold by Helen East (children's writer and storyteller) who heard it told many times in Iceland where it is very popular. The melody is adapted from a composition by Jón Asgeirsson.

To sing the song divide the children into two groups – one to sing the girl's part, the other to sing the troll's. The troll stands and gestures wildly with his hands, feet, and face, as he tries to call the girl's attention to each of them in turn. The girl sits and taps a regular beat with her foot as if rocking a cradle. Remember she must not look up at the troll.

The pronunciation of the Icelandic is given below the melody line.

Why the Grass Never Stops Growing – retold by Amoafi Kwapong (Ghanaian storyteller and musician) who heard it from a Ugandan storyteller. The words of the melody are in the Kimasaba language of Uganda, and Amoafi was told that 'Titi butitira' signifies the sound and movement of the bird, 'Karaere munywanyi wako' means roughly 'birds fly back into their own nests,' and 'kasindo, teruk, teruk, teruk' means 'grass, grow, grow, grow.' The opening and closing words of the story are in Swahili, the official language of Uganda.

When Amoafi tells this story, she dances a mime of the bird's movements – arms out for wings, head forward, and quick darting pecking movements on 'kasindo, teruk, teruk, teruk'.

The first bar of the song can be repeated throughout as a chorus, while the storyteller continues singing the rest of the song.

Pronunciation:

ae as in eye	*titi* sounds teetee
i as in feet	*u* as in too
o as in ode	

Kibungo – retold by Claudia da Silva (Brazilian storyteller/musician). This is a highly participative and lively story from the Brazilian Amazon. It reflects the racial mix found in the area – Kibungo, and Jabuti the trickster-heroine are both Amerindian characters, the songs are in Portuguese, and the dance is known in many parts of Brazil. It is danced as the story is told.

One child can be chosen to dance the part of Kibungo. As he or she takes one partner after

another it will soon become clear why Kibungo was left too exhausted to chase after Jabuti! The dance is very easy: during the chorus spin round with arms out, then rock from side to side; verse one – walk round in a circle, arms outstretched; verse two – hands on hips, tap or kick the feet out while turning round; verse three – hold right hands with partner, swing round one way, change hands and then swing round the other way.

The pronunciation of the words is given below the melody line.

The words of the first song mean 'Kibungo, wild beast of the forest'.

The Strange Visitor – retold by Helen East. Melody composed by Kevin Graal. There are versions of this story both in English and Scottish traditions. In England the original tune seems to have been lost, though in Scotland, the School of Scottish Studies has collected a tune from the travelling people.

When retelling this story the children can sing both the chorus 'And still she sat', and chant the Strange Visitor's replies to the old woman. The line 'From walking far, from walking far' should be chanted in a deep gruff voice, and the next line 'From staying up late and little food' in a high-pitched voice. Carry on in this way, alternating been high- and low-pitched voices. The whole narrative needs to be spoken rhythmically, each line occupying a four beat bar. The drum and woodblock indicated in the text mimic the entry of the Strange Visitor's bodily parts. The words 'for YOU' can crescendo slowly and ominously into a shout.

The Raja's Secret – retold by Niru Desai (Indian storyteller and poet). The song is in Gujarati and

the story is particularly popular in Gujarat, though it is known all over India.

The Raja's kantopi (pronounced kan-toe-pee) is a kind of headdress (topi) which covers the ears (kaan – ears). The instruments which give away his secret are the tabla – the popular two-piece drum, the sitar – a plucked string instrument, end-blown flute and tambourine. If these are not available you can substitute two differently pitched drums playing quaver beats, guitar or plucked violin, and recorder or Western flute. A drone accompaniment on the note D can also be added.

Pronunciation:
ah as in cheetah
bhai sounds ba-ee
e at the end of a word as in the French *é*
Manji sounds *Munjee*, but as it is a name, we have
   written it as it commonly appears in Roman
   script
o as in ode

Colin's Cattle – retold by Betsy Whyte. There are many tales about fairies which frequently show them in very different lights. Their jealousy here contrasts with the kindness of the fairy who came to the rescue in *The Finger Lock*.

The Lion on the Path – retold by Hugh Tracey with music transcribed by Andrew Tracey. The story comes from the Shona people of Zimbabwe, and the song is in the Karanga dialect.

The mbira is a small hand-held instrument with metal or wooden tongues which the player plucks with the thumbs or fingers. The mbira part given here can be played on the upper register of a piano, or on a xylophone – divide the music into parts for more than one player.

As a separate activity the players can be divided into two groups, one taking the part of the man, the other the rabbit. In order not to break the lion's trance, pass the mbira music from one group to the other by overlapping it. Another child could be chosen to be the lion who roars if the music is not gentle enough or if there are any breaks in it.

Pronunciation:
e as in ate	*u* as in too
i as in feet	*ai* as in eye

Toad and Donkey – adapted by Yvonne Charlton from versions told by Walter Jekyll in *Jamaican Song and Story* (Dover Publications) and by Louise Bennett-Coverley in *Anancy and Miss Lou* (Sangster's Book Stores Ltd, Jamaica). Again the children can be divided into two groups, one to be the donkey who gets more and more exhausted, while the frog remains fresh and cheerful through to the end.

The closing line 'Jack mandora me no choose none' is said to reassure the listeners that the story is not told against any of them.

All Skin and Bone – retold by Helen East. This is a variation on a well-known children's rhyme; the spoken line should be chanted rhythmically, and everyone can join in with the 'hoo ha' chorus. The last line should grow into a shout.

Little Cock Featherfrock – retold by Helen East. There are other versions of this story from Russia; some have different endings, and the blackbird is untypical. The melody was remembered by Valentina Coe who wrote the Russian words to it.

Remember to make the fox sing more enticingly each time he returns. The cat's song can be accompanied by a guitar or the children can mime playing the bandoura – a large lute with several strings from the Ukraine. Someone else can be the blackbird whistling along with the tune.

Pronunciation:
o as in ode
y when not next to a vowel sounds as in will
h in *eeh* sounds like a *very* soft version of the ch in
   Bach
zha sounds as in the French *jardin*.

The Little Bird and the Raja – retold by Nikhat Mohamed. There are many versions of this story especially in Bengal where the bird is said to be a tailor-bird. Nikhat's version is translated from Deehati (Village) Urdu and was learnt, as a child, from her (wet) nurse in Lucknow.

Some of the detail in the second half of the story has not been included as the symbolism would have been difficult to convey successfully in translation. When the bird is being prepared for the Raja to eat she makes out that she is being prepared for marriage with him i.e. when her throat is cut and the blood runs out, she sings 'I am dressed in red' (like a bride); when she is plucked she sings 'Now I am naked', and finally when she is fried she sings 'The drums and guns are sizzling and popping' (in celebration).

A guide to pronunciation is given with the melody. The *g* in *jug* is hard and forms a separate syllable.

Bouki Dances the Kokioko – retold by Diane Wolkstein (American storyteller). The story was told to her in Haiti where the dance was

demonstrated as follows: during the first four lines hold the body erect with right hand under right chest, sway upper chest from side to side – a bit like a cockerel; during the samba section clap hands and turn round and round.

Bouki and Malice appear as a trickster duo in many Haitian stories – Malice is the little clever one, Bouki is large, and slow on the uptake.

The Blind Beggar – retold by Helen East from an old Italian story which had lost its original melody. The substituted melody is from an Italian love song – *Amor dammi quel fazzolettino*. The new Italian words to the song are by Nicoletta Comano.

When telling this story, Helen usually stops at the point where the beggar finds the gold missing, and asks the children to suggest ways he can get it back, before continuing with his clever solution to the problem.

A pronunciation guide is given with the melody.

Mr Hawk and Mother Hen – retold by Amoafi Kwapong. Her first language is Twi, and this story is from the Akan tradition of Ghana.

When Amoafi sings the song, she accompanies each syllable with a drum beat which matches the tonal inflections of the voice, so the drum is in effect speaking the words. Try this on a drum by pressing the drumskin with one hand as you strike it with the other. This will raise the pitch.

The children sing the repeated 'sensensa', and dance like chickens by making their arms into wings (arms doubled up, hands in front of shoulders, elbows out to each side) and flapping them up and down against their sides to make a slapping sound on each syllable.

A pronunciation guide is given with the melody.

The Boy who Lived with the Bears – retold by Joseph Bruchac III. The story is from the Iroquois tradition. The song could be sung first by the storyteller and then by the children imitating the voices of the animals. The words are vocables which cannot be translated.

Accompany the song as follows: sing it through three times each time it appears in the story.

First time: voice only, let the voice fall off downwards from the last note.

Second time:

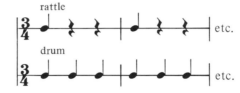

Third time: as for second time but louder.
Last four bars:

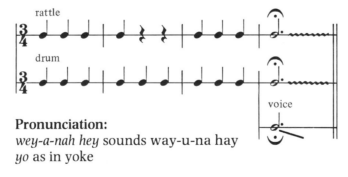

Pronunciation:
wey-a-nah hey sounds way-u-na hay
yo as in yoke

The Singing Sack – retold by Helen East from a traditional Andaluçian story. The story is also known in a similar version in Tanzania. The original song was lost and this substitute is a traditional Andaluçian lullaby (*Mi niño chiquito se quiere dormir*). The pronunciation is given below the melody line.

Sambalele – retold by Claudia da Silva. This Brazilian story is a variation on the well-known tar-baby theme. The song is in Portuguese, and the children could tackle the chorus first until they are ready to join in with the verses. Simple percussion on the offbeat could be added, and the children might try making up a mocking dance.

A pronunciation guide is given below the melody.

Annancy, Puss and Ratta – a traditional Jamaican story adapted by Yvonne Charlton from versions told by Walter Jekyll in *Jamaican Song and Story* (Dover Publications) and by Louise Bennett-Coverley in *Anancy and Miss Lou* (Sangster's Book Stories Ltd, Jamaica).

Since the story is so short, a group of children could be chosen to sing Annancy's fiddle music throughout the telling, getting faster and faster as the story goes on.

A Tale for our Time – by Helen East. This is the only song-story in the book which has never been told before. Helen dedicates it to all those who live in cities, and offers the shadow and its song as friendly charms to ward off the scarey monsters which have prowled through these pages. She also hopes it will encourage you and the children to make up your own song-stories – they can be old songs within new stories, old stories round new songs, a variation on a theme, or something completely original.

The children will find the song easy to sing and the accompanying actions easy to dance. Let them be as inventive as they like – add new verses, new actions, or different endings. Take it away and make it part of your own oral tradition.

Acknowledgements

The compiler and publishers wish to give special thanks to the following: Belle and Sheila Stewart, and Ian and Roy MacGregor for permission to adapt Andra Stewart's retelling of *The Finger Lock*; The School of Scottish Studies for general advice and material, and a transcription of the Gaelic words to the song in *The Lonely Mermaid*, and for supplying the original tune to *The Finger Lock*; Bairbre ni Fhloinn and Professor Almquist of the Department of Irish Folklore, Dublin, for advice and suggestions of Irish material; Thorgerdur Ingólfsdóttir, Bergljót Jónsdóttir and Haida Petersdottür for help with Icelandic material, and Jón Asgeirsson for permission to adapt from a composition the song used in *The Night Troll*; The Folklore Society for information on *Annancy, Puss and Ratta* and *Toad and Donkey*, and for permission to use the accompanying melodies, and Yvonne Charlton for adapting both stories; Nicoletta Comano and Carmen Leone for help with the Italian words and pronunciation of the song in *The Blind Beggar*; James Riordan for research and Valentina Coe for the Russian words and tune to *Little Cock Featherfrock*; Georgina Legoretta and Geoff Wilson for help with the Spanish words and pronunciation of the song to *The Singing Sack*; and finally the staff and pupils of Down Lane Junior School and St Osyth C of E Primary School for their enthusiastic help in trying out illustration techniques for the book.

Grateful thanks are also due to the following who have contributed their copyright material:

Jón Asgeirsson for the original tune to *The Night Troll*.

Chandrika Bheda for *Bhambhutia*.

Joseph Bruchac III for *The Boy who Lived with the Bears* and *Gluskabi and the Wind Eagle*.

Valentina Coe for the Russian words to *Little Cock Featherfrock*.

Vivienne Corringham for *Momo-taro-san*.

Claudia da Silva for *Kibungo* and *Sambalele*.

Niru Desai for *The Raja's Secret*.

Helen East for *All Skin and Bone, A Tale for Our Time, The Blind Beggar, The Night Troll, The Singing Sack, Little Cock Featherfrock, The Strange Visitor*.

The Folklore Society for the songs to *Annancy, Puss and Ratta*, and *Toad and Donkey*.

Folktracks and Sound Post Publications for the original tune to *Did the Rum Do?* © Seamus Ennis/ Folktracks and Sound Post Publications.

Kevin Graal for *Did the Rum Do?* and the melody to *The Strange Visitor*.

Folo Graff for *Spider the Drummer*.

Sandra Kerr for the melody to *Quilla Bung*.

Amoafi Kwapong for *Mr Hawk and Mother Hen* and *Why the Grass Never Stops Growing*.

Nikhat Mohamed for *The Little Bird and the Raja*.

Routledge and Kegan Paul for *The Lion on the Path* and *Nyangara* from *The Lion on the Path and other African Stories* by Hugh Tracey, © 1967.

Bryce Whyte for *Colin's Cattle* and *The Lonely Mermaid* by Betsy Whyte.

Diane Wolkstein for *Bouki Dances the Kokioko*, retold in *The Magic Orange Tree and other Haitian Folktales* published by Shocken Books and Cambridge University Press.

Index of song titles and first lines